D1103147

50000000127114

A MESSAGE FROM CHICKEN HOUSE

Siblings Sal and Asha live in a haunted house, but they've got a lot more than ghosts to cope with . . . There's a group of charming, lovable, maddening friends – and a romance between two very different boys to drive them to distraction! Not to mention the real secret behind the haunting, which won't stay hidden for ever . . .

Fran Hart was the runaway winner of the Chairman's Choice Prize in our *Times*/Chicken House Children's Fiction Competition in 2020 for this funny, engaging and relatable novel. After all, we are all 'the other ones' sometimes: misfits who find friendship and comfort in one another against the world.

BARRY CUNNINGHAM
Publisher
Chicken House

The Other Ones

FRAN HART

Chicken House

2 Palmer Street, Frome, Somerset BA11 1DS
www.chickenhousebooks.com

Text © Fran Hart 2022

First published in Great Britain in 2022
Chicken House
2 Palmer Street
Frome, Somerset BA11 1DS
United Kingdom
www.chickenhousebooks.com

Chicken House/Scholastic Ireland, 89E Lagan Road, Dublin Industrial Estate,
Glasnevin, Dublin D11 HP5F, Republic of Ireland

Cover and interior design by Micaela Alcaino
Typeset by Dorchester Typesetting Group Ltd
Printed and bound in Great Britain by CPI Group (UK) Ltd, Croydon CR0 4YY

FSC
www.fsc.org
MIX
Paper from
responsible sources
FSC® C171272

1 3 5 7 9 10 8 6 4 2

British Library Cataloguing in Publication data available.

PB ISBN 978-1-913696-32-0
eISBN 978-1-915026-07-1

For Caroline

Let me tell you what it's like to be haunted.

You don't remember the first time you realized it wasn't normal: living with ghosts in your house. But the ghosts are more a part of your life than any of your friends. Than anyone at all. They are a constant, chilling presence.

You see them everywhere you turn. They are in the peeling wallpaper, in the stained floor, in the scratches on the doors. They are in the ceilings laced with cobwebs. They are woven into the very threads of your existence. And every so often, they tug on its strings, and threaten to pull it apart.

Your house is not a home. It is tall, and dark, and imposing. Even on the sunniest days, its shadow spreads further than it should. Everybody knows your house is haunted. They have seen the crumbling walls and the decaying window frames. They can imagine ghosts making themselves at home inside.

People shrink from it. And, in the dead of night, you shrink from it too.

CHAPTER ONE

Number seventeen Yew Tree Lane was a tall and rickety house with grey wood panelling that was beginning to sag and rot. The roof was unusually pointy, formed of two sloping apexes, and the walls appeared as if they were being swallowed by the sprawling mass of ivy that covered them.

The inhabitants of Holden refused to go near it. There had once been neighbours, but the houses next door both sat empty now. The postman threw the post over the gate, which had fallen from its frame and sunk into the ground. The locals quickened their steps as they passed by the end of the drive. Even the trees that lined the property's perimeter seemed fearful. They strained against their roots, their long limbs stretching away from the house's walls.

Sal had lived there since he was born. When he was a

boy, his mother had told him not to leave his room at night. The house wasn't safe, she said, once the sun had gone down. In the bright light of day, he and his sister – Asha – played at slaying ghosts. In their imaginations the ghosts cowered before them. They could be beaten away with wooden spoons and old umbrellas.

At nearly seventeen years old, Sal knew the things that haunted them couldn't always be defeated. He had learnt to keep his head down, to live in their shadow. If he tried hard enough to be ordinary then maybe, one day, he would be.

It was a Sunday morning, the 4th of October, one month into the new school year. The first of the autumn leaves were beginning to fall from the trees and, down by the farm, the pumpkins were starting to swell in the patch. The corn in the field across the lane had reached shoulder height, and soon nobody would be able to see over its swaying, golden stems. But Sal would remember the day as *the day the doorbell rang.*

He was huddled on the end of the sofa when it happened, scooping cereal from the box straight into his mouth and staring at the old television screen as it cycled through endless reruns of old cartoons, screen flickering and buzzing with static sounds. At the peal of the doorbell he paused, hand halfway to his mouth, and turned to frown through the front windows. There was no sign of a car on the lane outside. There wasn't even a delivery van, driven by one of those rare drivers who hadn't yet heard the house was haunted and was still willing to climb over the broken gate and trek the fifty metres up the drive. Sal stood up and approached the windows, attempting to peer through the ivy that covered them. The porch, and whoever was standing on it, was shielded from view.

He remained frozen in place. The doorbell rang again. And then again.

Sal made a half-hearted attempt at brushing the cereal crumbs from his hoodie. The floorboards in the hall creaked beneath his bare feet as he padded towards the front door. He looked through the stained-glass window in its centre and was met with the sight of a strangely fuzzy silhouette. Glancing behind him, he checked the hallway was empty before he unlocked the latches and opened the door.

Early morning sunshine poured through the ivy that hung over the porch. Dappled light seeped into the house, fingers reaching for the gloom in its corners.

The boy on the doorstep was around Sal's own age. But the similarities ended there. He was one of the strangest-looking boys Sal had ever seen, wrapped in a thick furry coat so large it dwarfed his slender frame. The rust-coloured fur contrasted dramatically with his fair skin and large pale grey eyes. He was peering out at Sal from beneath a knitted hat, complete with ear flaps and long plaited tassels. Standing before him, in his old hoodie and jogging bottoms, Sal felt seriously underdressed.

The boy's face broke into an ear-splitting smile. 'You must be Salem.'

Sal briefly considered correcting his pronunciation. It

was pronounced Sah-lim. The boy on the doorstep was calling him Say-lem, like the black cat in *Sabrina the Teenage Witch*. And he seemed to be getting a kick out of it. Which was annoying.

'It's Sal,' Sal said instead. He had always hated his name, chosen by his Egyptian father. He was yet to meet anyone who pronounced it right and, even when they did, it didn't suit him.

The boy beamed at him. He was clutching a casserole dish in his hands and he held it out to Sal with the air of someone laying down a sacrifice at an altar.

'I prefer Salem,' the boy told him. 'It's a beautiful name.'

He blinked owlishly at Sal, who stood in silence, arms folded, unsure how to react to this boy who dressed like a woodland animal and spoke like a grandmother. The boy squeezed past him into the house and, when Sal still did not accept the proffered casserole dish, set it carefully down on the hallway table. He smiled again.

'That will need refrigerating.'

Sal frowned down at the dish. It reminded him of when his dad had died, five years before. Their neighbours had overcome their fear of the house for long enough to bring them cards and flowers. The fridge had been packed with dishes that didn't belong to them, full of food that they couldn't bring themselves to eat.

Sal cleared his throat. 'Who *are* you?'

'Oh.' The boy looked surprised, as if it hadn't occurred to him that Sal might actually want to know who he was. He held out a hand for him to shake. 'Hi, I'm Pax.'

Pax's enjoyment of Sal's own name suddenly made a little more sense.

Sal accepted his hand reluctantly. Pax's skin was cold against his own. Sal let go as quickly as could possibly be deemed polite, and instantly regretted having taken his hand at all when Pax took it as an invitation to meander down the hall, looking around with interest. He ran a finger along the twisted wood of the banisters, peered at the dusty chandelier overhead and examined the faded pattern of the wallpaper.

'I thought it would be spookier,' he announced.

Sal couldn't understand why he was disappointed. Their house could have been pictured under the dictionary definition of *spooky*. It had been standing for over a century, and was beginning to fall apart at the seams. It hadn't been decorated since the 1920s. The ceilings were high and the windows were narrow. There were cobwebs in the corners and the floorboards creaked even when nobody was standing on them.

At the other end of the hall, Pax was leaning in to peer at the family photographs that lined the wall. The pictures were faded and dusty in their tarnished frames – long-forgotten snapshots that Sal, Asha and their mum passed by every day without ever really noticing. Sal and Asha as children, opening Christmas presents, their faces bright and smiling. Their mother, with her arms wrapped around them at the beach, her pale skin a stark contrast to their own, nearly glowing in the sun. His father, aged thirty-four, dark eyes staring impressively out of the frame.

It was the last photo taken before he had died.

'Have you met the other inhabitants?' Pax asked.

'Well, yeah,' Sal said, frowning. 'They're my family.'

'Oh, no.' Pax chuckled. He turned back around to face him and lowered his voice conspiratorially. 'No. I meant . . . *you know* . . . the *other* ones.'

Sal didn't answer. He knew perfectly well that Pax was talking about ghosts. But when he didn't have anything he wanted to say, he liked to conserve energy and not say anything at all. He had been well into his teenage years before it occurred to him that he was unusual in that regard, and that most of the world shied away from prolonged periods of silence.

His silence did not seem to bother this boy, but that was probably because he was so busy filling it.

'We just moved to the village,' Pax said. 'Me and Mum. I've been dying to find out more about the haunted house, of course. Mum said it was probably nonsense and she wanted to bring the casserole, but I said I'd do it. I helped make it.'

He turned back to Sal and watched him expectantly.

'Um . . .' Sal folded his arms across his chest. 'Thanks?'

'It's no trouble.' Pax shook his head. 'I wanted to meet you anyway, before I start school. I've heard all about you.'

Sal thought that was unlikely. There wasn't a soul in the entire village who knew *all about him*. Apart from maybe Asha, and she didn't make a habit of talking to strangers. Especially strangers as strange as this one.

'OK . . .' He took a step towards the boy in the hope of

herding him back towards the front door.

Pax stood his ground. He pulled off his hat and a tumble of light-blond curls cascaded down to skim his jawline. 'I don't have any friends yet.'

'Right.' Sal sidestepped him and opened the door. Not having any friends wasn't something you just admitted to. He half wondered why Pax was starting a new school a month into the autumn term, but didn't want to encourage conversation by asking. 'Well . . . thanks for the casserole.'

Pax twisted his hat between his hands. 'You can bring the dish back any time.'

Sal nodded, already dreading doing so. He opened the door wider, and the wind swept in, scattering autumn leaves across the doormat.

'We're in the cottage by the church,' Pax said. He pointed past the gargoyles that framed the porch, and down the driveway towards the lane. 'I'm sure my mum would love to meet you.'

'OK.'

'Well.' Pax crammed his hat back on to his head, finally taking the hint and stepping over the threshold. He patted one of the gargoyles appreciatively on the head. 'I'll look out for you at school. Mrs Helliwell at number twenty-one said you'd be in my year.'

Sal barely resisted the urge to roll his eyes. Mrs Helliwell lived down the lane in a small cottage with a large vegetable garden, which she shared with several very fat tabby cats. She liked to think she knew everything about everyone and enjoyed sharing her knowledge with anyone who would listen. He wondered if Pax had delivered casseroles to everyone along the lane, gathering gossip along with thank-yous.

'I'll leave you my number,' Pax continued. He rested a hand on the door to prevent Sal from closing it and began rummaging around in his pocket. 'You might need it.'

He produced a tattered scrap of card from his pocket and handed it to Sal, beaming at him, as if he thought this might seal the deal on their new and very much non-existent friendship.

'Great,' Sal said, as the uncomfortable beginnings of guilt stirred in the pit of his stomach. Asha would have told him he was being mean. He caved and forced a smile. 'So I'll see you around.'

Pax finally stepped away from the porch, casting a reluctant glance over his shoulder as he did so. He gave Sal a little wave and Sal smiled tightly back at him, watching him retreat down the drive.

'Salem?' Pax called out, turning around once he had nearly reached the gate. He was a good twenty metres away and his voice was almost lost in the wind.

'What?'

'I could help you with the hauntings,' Pax shouted, lifting his hands to his mouth in order to help him project his voice. 'I'm good with ghosts.'

Sal closed the door behind him, and took extra care sliding shut the bolts. He looked down at the scrap of card in his hands. *Pax Delaney* was scrawled on it in a loopy cursive. Beneath that there was a phone number, and beneath *that* was a roughly doodled ghost.

He stuffed it in the back pocket of his jogging bottoms and hid the casserole dish in the back of the fridge, where he didn't have to look at it.

The sun was setting when Asha got home from work that evening. Sal saw her coming and opened the front door. She was clutching half a dozen shopping bags and her breath was misting in the frosty air. She strode straight through to the kitchen, flung the bags on the countertop and untied her apron with the fervour of someone finally freeing themselves of their shackles.

Asha was barely a year older than Sal, but she considered herself infinitely wiser. Sal found this annoying but had to admit she had a point. Even as kids, she had always been the smart one. When Sal was just about old enough to read, Asha would spend days on end curled up with books and scrawling stories on notepaper. She had been moved ahead a school year as soon as she got to Holden High.

She had aced her exams in spring and been offered a place at King's College London to study English Lit. She hadn't told anyone, but Sal had found the letter neatly folded inside a prospectus in her desk drawer. The shiny booklet was so well thumbed that the paper had turned as soft as tissue and the corners turned up temptingly at the edges. There was a laughing girl on the cover, white with blonde hair, carrying a backpack and looking every inch the exact opposite of his sister. When Sal had asked her about university, she'd told him she'd decided not to go.

Asha worked full-time at the local shop now instead. She hated everything about it, from the sickly green shade of the apron to the long hours spent stacking tins under fluorescent lights and watching the clock drag its hands towards home time.

Sal watched her pile food on to the kitchen counter: cheese strings and chocolate milk, pizzas and cookie dough, hot chilli sauce and cans upon cans of Diet Coke. When she opened the fridge, she paused, confronted with the sight of the floral casserole dish. She poked at it suspiciously. Their mum spent all her time working and when she did have a chance to cook, it usually ended up burnt.

'Why is there actual human food in here?'

'We had a visitor,' Sal said.

'What?' Asha looked panicked. 'Who? Why?'

'Some weird kid.' Sal helped himself to a cheese string. 'His family just moved in down the lane.'

Asha seemed to relax at that. She moved the dish to one side and began piling the shopping in around it. 'Haven't they heard we're haunted yet?'

'They heard,' Sal said. 'That's why he came.'

'Oh dear.'

Sal nodded. 'Yeah.'

She pulled the casserole dish from the fridge and they both stood and stared at it doubtfully. When Asha pulled back the clingfilm, the room was filled with the rich buttery scent of roasted squash and thyme. Sal's mouth started watering.

'Well, put it in the oven,' she said decisively. 'I'm bored of pizza.'

They ate on the sofa, curled up under blankets and shovelling the hot home-cooked food into their mouths with enthusiasm. It was a cold evening, and Asha lit a fire in the grate, casting the room in a warm orange glow. The house, for once, felt almost like a normal home.

'I'm glad you met this kid,' Asha announced, once she had finished. She set her empty plate down next to her feet on the coffee table and stretched out her arms above her head, yawning like a contented kitten. 'I like him.'

Sal snorted. 'He's really weird.'

Asha just smiled. 'So are you.'

CHAPTER TWO

Sal awoke late on Monday morning. He made a habit of waking up late on school days, because then he didn't have to spend as long wishing he didn't have to go. School bored him, and he spent most of his time there staring out of the window. He could skate by with mid-range grades without very much effort, and that was how he liked it. Unlike Asha, he had never dreamt of attending university.

Asha was already in the kitchen when he got down-stairs, eating a bowl of Cheerios, with a book in one hand and her spoon in the other. She rolled her eyes at the sight of his outfit (ripped jeans and a baggy black hoodie) and reached out to attempt to fix his hair.

Sal shook her off.

He had inherited his father's hair: thick, dark and tangled. It was good hair, according to Asha, but Sal didn't know what to do with it. Mostly he left it alone and it grew straight up in a strange, wavy pompadour style. He had heavy, brooding eyebrows, which made him look as though he was always scowling, even when he was in a good mood.

People liked to tell Sal that he had a *bad attitude*. He thought this had more to do with his wardrobe and unintentional scowl than his actual personality, but it did not particularly bother him, because he enjoyed being left alone. Asha stopped trying to improve his appearance and stabbed at the soggy remnants of her cereal. She was already dressed in her work uniform, her apron crisply ironed and her long dark braids pulled back into a neat ponytail.

'You're going to give us a bad reputation,' she said.

'We already have one,' Sal said. 'Our house is haunted.'

They were interrupted by a loud *ah-wooooo*-ing noise coming from the hallway. Asha pointed her spoon at Sal, dripping milk on to the floor as she did so.

'You're getting that.'

There was a rapping on the front door as she spoke and Sal sighed before heading into the hall. Dirk was one of the only people in the village willing to approach the house. He was also Sal's only real friend and enjoyed announcing his presence by howling through the letterbox.

Dirk stepped inside as soon as Sal opened the door, looking around hopefully. 'Hey. Is Asha in?'

'No,' Asha called. 'She's not at home.'

Sal grabbed his backpack from the floor and bundled the other boy out of the house before he could head through to the kitchen.

Dirk was always very loud and often exceptionally annoying. He was also determined to be Sal's friend, despite being in the year above him at school. He was one of the only people who Sal had never managed to shake off.

Sal wasn't sure if their friendship was a result of actual compatibility or just sheer stubbornness on Dirk's part. But he was grateful for it all the same. If nothing else, Dirk's constant presence meant Sal never had to sit alone in the high school cafeteria. Being friends with him had become a habit he had stopped trying to break.

The previous night's gale had left the driveway covered in leaves. They kicked through them and Dirk lit them both cigarettes as they reached the gate.

'Good weekend?' he asked.

'Weird,' Sal said, remembering Pax's visit. He glanced behind them to check Asha wasn't watching from the windows as he exhaled smoke and flicked ash on to the ground. 'Very weird.'

'And how's my future wife?' Dirk asked. He glanced back too, eyes longing as they lingered on the house.

Sal had been enduring Dirk's crush on Asha since they were twelve years old. Five years on, and it didn't show any signs of waning. Asha was, and always had been, thoroughly uninterested.

'Still not in love with you.'

Dirk clapped him on the back. '*Dude,*' he said effusively, 'it's only a matter of time.'

Holden High had once been a stately home, with great stone steps and a fountain in the grounds. Then it had been a fancy boarding school, until the 1950s, when a fire had ravaged its walls. Now it was a dilapidated high school, half cheap new plasterboard and half ancient stone – marked, in some places, with the black ghosts of the fire. The ceiling leaked and the classrooms had draughty windows and rattling radiators which did little to keep out the autumn chill. The once grand fountain was dry, used as a repository for cigarette butts and sweet wrappers, and as a place for teenagers to sit as they kissed.

The students in the lower years wore crisp blazers and ties. The sixth-formers could wear what they wanted but they had a kind of uniform of their own that everybody always stuck to. People dressed plainly, in jeans and T-shirts mostly. If you put in too much effort, people laughed at you behind your back.

Holden was a sleepy little village, but the high school had a reputation for bad behaviour. Sal thought this was inevitable, because its students had been left with no other options. The nearest town was a forty-minute drive away and no buses stopped at the only bus stop. There were no nightclubs for them to go to on a Friday night, no pub where the landlord didn't know half their parents. Even the park was surrounded by tall iron railings and carefully locked up at eight p.m.

Everything bad that was going to happen was, quite obviously, going to happen at school.

'Or in the woods,' Dirk pointed out, when Sal raised this theory. 'Talking of which, did you hear about Jacob and Elsie?'

'No.' Sal grimaced. 'And I don't want to.'

They were in the cafeteria, eating lukewarm lasagne at a table filled with Dirk's other friends, who were all talking very loudly and with their mouths full. The majority of them were Year 13 boys to whom Sal, by mutual agreement, barely spoke. They didn't have much in common. Two of them had begun a rowdy game of arm-wrestling at the other end of the table.

Dirk turned to one of the arm-wrestling boys, rising half out of his seat to attract his attention. 'Yo, Matt,' he hollered at the top of his voice. 'Did you hear about Elsie Ward?'

Elsie stalked past as he spoke and the entire table descended into hoots of laughter. She narrowed her eyes at them and Sal pulled an apologetic face in return. He sat next to Elsie in English. She lent him pens and gave him gum, liked rock bands and incessantly encouraged him to get an eyebrow piercing. She was nice. He wished, for a moment, that he were sitting somewhere else.

At the other end of the cafeteria, he caught sight of Pax alone at a table. He was wearing a raggedy yellow cardigan, which seemed to consist solely of loose threads knotted together, and made him look as if he had been swallowed by a ball of wool. The students nearest him were watching him cautiously, and a group of boys behind him were laughing at his cardigan.

Sal would have found the situation impossibly awkward, but Pax appeared perfectly content. He was looking around in mild interest, as if he were at a dinner party and hadn't quite decided who he wanted to talk to first.

His gaze landed on Sal, who realized he had been staring and immediately ducked his head.

When Sal got home from school that afternoon, he found the photograph of his father had fallen off the wall. He picked it up and frowned back at the eyes staring out at him, an exact match of his own. Sal had only been eleven when he died. He'd crossed a road without looking one day, and never came home.

But the house hadn't let him go. There was something about their house that held on to things lost, and brought memories alive. Sal's mother had a theory that nobody who lived there ever really died.

His mother was an artist. She painted swirling abstract pieces in gloomy colours on big canvases. Privately, Sal didn't like them. He thought they looked like storm clouds, on the verge of breaking open and unleashing unfathomable amounts of rain. But they had once sold for a lot of money. She had met Sal's father at a big art show in a fancy London gallery when they both reached for the same glass of champagne. They were married six months later and moved to the countryside, to live in a house already rumoured to be haunted. They hadn't believed the rumours, back then.

Since Sal's dad had died, his mother had spent most of her time in her own head. She had stopped painting, and the art studio in the attic went unused. She had stopped talking about Sal's dad too, or whatever it was that was left of him. The remnants of his existence that kept her awake at night, unable to sleep. If Sal or Asha tried to ask questions, it annoyed her. After years of persisting, they had learnt not to ask.

Sal rehung the photo on the wall, and went through to the kitchen to feed his caffeine addiction. His mum had left an empty coffee mug on the counter, and Sal refilled it absent-mindedly while making his own. He made it almost painfully strong, knowing he wouldn't sleep anyway.

CHAPTER THREE

That night Sal startled awake and sat bolt upright in bed. His heart was racing, his mouth dry. The blurriness of sleep had been usurped by a sudden sharp alertness. An awareness that the darkness surrounding him had changed. That somewhere within it, something was moving.

That was when he heard them. The ghostly voices. For months, they had sounded in the dead of night. Though the words were muffled, he knew they were spiked with hatred; cold, bitter echoes of the past. He kept his eyes squeezed closed and fisted his hands in the sheets. There came the sound of footsteps thundering down the stairs. Sal held his breath, listening intently. He heard the sound of the front door being dragged open, and the reverberating bang of it being pulled closed at force.

It was a little after midnight, and his room would have been pitch-black without the weak grey light of the moon seeping in through the dusty windowpanes. Sleep stolen from him, he pushed back the covers. He couldn't see the front door from his window, but the front porch below was shadowy and still. The only sign of movement was the ivy twisting in the wind. His bedroom window was cracked, and the chill seeping through it was enough to raise the hairs on his arms and legs. His heart was still pounding as he wrapped himself in joggers and a hoodie before heading downstairs.

In the dead of night, the house felt changed. Every shadow was foreign and unfamiliar, every shape blurring and morphing before his eyes. There was little wind outside but the old bones of the house creaked and groaned. The darkness was alive.

There was no sign of movement in the hallway, but he took the stairs two at a time, unwilling to linger. In the shadowy half-light, he pulled on a scuffed pair of trainers and unlocked the door, fingers faltering on the latches.

As he stepped out into the night, he heard footsteps again, this time at the top of the stairs behind him. He pulled the front door gently closed and set off at a jog down the drive. Behind him, a light flicked on. He turned to see light pouring from the windows of the attic. In the darkness, the two windowpanes were like narrowed yellow eyes. The night was bitterly cold, but he sucked in great lungfuls of the icy air, letting it burn his throat and bring tears to his eyes.

22

He vaulted the broken gate at the end of the drive and by the time he reached the lane he was sprinting. The yew trees that lined it were ancient. Their gnarled branches arched overhead, forming a tunnel of darkness through which the moonlight could not hope to break. He climbed the stile at the end, crossed the cornfield and began his usual circuit of the village, focusing on nothing but the thud of his feet on the ground and the steady pounding of his heart in his chest.

Sal loved being out at night. And when he couldn't sleep, he ran.

Holden seemed less oppressive at night, and Sal could almost imagine he was somewhere else. The village was overrun with rabbits, and once the sun had set they appeared from their burrows and claimed the sleepy little village as their own. On every unkempt lawn, on every grass verge, on the banks of the river, their soft round silhouettes appeared as far as the eye could see. They looked up curiously as he passed, tiny noses twitching in the cold night air, before deciding he was no threat and returning to their grazing.

The rabbits were not the only creatures out that night.

Sal slowed to a halt in the very centre of the village, and bent over to catch his breath, staring at the cobblestones. When he raised his head, he was greeted by the sight of a small glowing light amid the headstones of the local church. Sitting on a great tombstone, holding his knees to his chest and staring up at the moon, was Pax.

Sal kicked the cobblestones in frustration and walked

away. All he wanted was to be alone. He made it halfway across the square before his curiosity got the better of him. He hesitated, scowling at the sky.

'For god's sake,' he muttered under his breath.

He turned and set off at a jog back to the graveyard.

Pax looked up at him as he approached, his eyes widening. The light was coming from a tiny candlelit lantern at the head of the tomb and, on the ground at his feet, there was a picnic basket. He was wearing his fur coat again, over what appeared to be a vibrantly patterned pair of pyjama bottoms. There was a very thick knitted scarf slung around his neck in a violent shade of orange. He was nibbling absent-mindedly on a sandwich.

Sal sat down next to him, catching his breath. It misted in great clouds in the air between them.

'Why are you so weird?' he asked.

Pax seemed to consider this for a moment. He swallowed, set his sandwich on the mossy stone of the tomb and brushed a smattering of crumbs out of the fur of his coat.

'I don't know,' he said eventually. 'I always thought I was normal.'

'You're having a picnic in a graveyard.'

Pax blinked at him disconcertingly with those wide pale eyes. He smiled, leant over and rummaged in his picnic basket.

'Peanut butter sandwich?'

Sal's stomach rumbled at the words, and he accepted the sandwich with a half-hearted show of reluctance. It

24

was made on soft white bread and cut into neat triangles with the crusts carefully removed.

'My dad thought I was strange,' Pax said. 'That's why he left.'

Sal swallowed his mouthful of sandwich too quickly, and it dragged slowly and painfully down his throat.

'I'm not supposed to know that,' Pax said, lifting a hand to his mouth as if surprised the words had left it. Suddenly shaken from his dreamy demeanour, he fixed Sal with a stern expression. 'Don't tell anyone.'

'I mean. You're not *that* strange.'

Pax raised his eyebrows.

'And, hey,' Sal said, taking another bite of the sandwich. 'At least you're not boring.'

'That's what my mum says,' Pax said brightly.

They sat in silence for a moment, eating in the darkness and looking up at the stars above their heads. They looked like tiny pinpricks in the dark blanket of the sky, letting light through from some faraway place beyond.

'My dad's gone too,' Sal said.

Pax blinked at him. 'Gone where?'

'I don't know.' The peanut butter was sticking to the roof of his mouth, making it difficult to speak. 'He's dead.'

When he glanced back at Pax, the boy was staring at him.

'Don't worry,' Sal said, 'it happened five years ago.'

'I'm sorry,' Pax said, holding his gaze.

Sal turned away and looked out at the graveyard instead. The church loomed over them, its silhouette a black hole against the moonlit sky. Its proximity made him uneasy.

'What are you doing here?' Sal asked, when Pax made no further attempts at conversation.

'I live here,' Pax said.

Sal looked around at the rows of gravestones, and back at Pax. 'You *what*?'

Pax pointed through the trees opposite them, to a crumbling stone cottage beyond. There was a light on over the porch. 'We live in the old graveyard keeper's cottage,' he said. 'So this is basically my garden.'

Sal squinted over at it through the darkness. He squinted back at Pax. Then he reached out and poked him, hard, in the ribs.

'Hey!' Pax squirmed and batted his hand away. 'What was that for?'

'I thought I must be imagining you,' Sal told him. 'I was just checking you're real.'

'Because I'm too good to be true?' Pax suggested.

Sal snorted. 'Something like that.'

Pax leant a touch closer on the tombstone, the candle-light casting his face half into flickering shadow. 'Why are *you* here? Are the ghosts keeping you up?'

Sal shrugged, unwilling to talk. He set down his sandwich, head suddenly full once more with the other-worldly noises.

Pax leant closer still, lowering his voice to a whisper, as if someone among the graves might be listening. 'I really think I could help.' He dusted a few lingering sandwich crumbs from his fingers. 'If you just tell me a bit more about it.'

Sal frowned at him. 'What makes you think you could help?'

'I know a lot about ghosts,' Pax said. 'I've read all the books. Seen all the shows. Everything. It's a passion of mine.'

Sal didn't think reading books and watching *Ghostbusters* qualified Pax to give him any kind of advice. He pushed himself up off the tombstone and kicked away the dead leaves at his feet. His head was unwillingly filled with images of the rotting skeletons of the corpses buried below. He imagined the roots of trees squeezing through eye sockets and winding around ribcages.

'I don't need your help.'

He strode away towards the graveyard gate, legs still burning from the run, and uncomfortably conscious of Pax's gaze on his back.

'Salem?' the boy called after him, when he was nearly too far away to hear.

'What?' Sal asked, not turning back to face him.

Pax's voice was rich with amusement. 'You still have my casserole dish.'

Sal turned back around and stuck his middle finger up at the boy, but tempered it with a smile. When he was halfway home he realized, with a surge of annoyance, that he was still smiling.

When Sal awoke the next morning it was freezing cold and he was still dressed in the clothes he had worn for his run. The sun was rising, and light was seeping in through the dust-streaked window, turning the walls of his room a soft orange-pink. When he padded downstairs to the kitchen, Asha was already there. Sal and his mum were both normally night owls, and Asha was the only person in the house who voluntarily rose before midday. Eggshells littered the countertop, and she was stirring a bowl of batter with such vigour that drops of it kept flying from the spoon.

'Pancakes?' Sal asked hopefully.

Asha cooked when she was stressed, and not always with good results. But her pancakes usually turned out perfectly. She tipped the first of the batter into the pan, and Sal's stomach immediately rumbled.

'How did you sleep?' she asked, passing him a cup of coffee.

Sal took the coffee and inhaled gratefully. It was exactly as he liked it. Strong enough that it tasted like dirt and hot enough that it made his entire body shudder when it hit his throat.

'I couldn't,' he said. 'I went out for a run.'

Asha's brow furrowed. She grabbed the spatula that hung above the hob and began poking at the edges of the pancake. 'In the middle of the night? Sounds like a good way to get murdered.'

'You're assuming someone could catch up with me,' Sal pointed out, with a grin. He helped himself to a plate from the kitchen cupboard.

Asha snorted, and flipped the pancake with such force

that it got stuck on the kitchen ceiling for a second, before falling back into the pan. She poked at it consideringly and slid it on to Sal's plate. 'Enjoy.'

CHAPTER FOUR

The casserole dish sat, scrubbed and shining, on the kitchen table, a constant reminder of the boy Sal was trying to avoid. For a full week he let Asha nag him about returning it, before hiding it at the back of the highest cupboard and telling her he had taken it back.

If Sal happened to pass Pax in the school corridors, he lowered his gaze and pretended he hadn't seen him. They shared an art class, where Sal was careful to sit at the opposite end of the room, leaving Pax alone at his spot by the radiator. If Pax turned around and caught his eye, Sal simply nodded and returned to his work. Ignoring him, however, was not an easy task. As the temperature dropped, the boy's outfits grew steadily more outlandish. He appeared to be using the cold weather as an excuse to layer all the strangest things in his wardrobe.

He wore corduroy trousers in bright colours, and cardigans with elbow patches over floral shirts, or oversized jumpers over leggings and wellies. He had a habit of keeping his hats on indoors and always gave the impression of being perpetually cosy and utterly content. Heads turned when he walked down the school corridors. He was also, always, alone.

It was a Monday morning, a week after Pax had arrived at Holden High. It was raining hard, the water soaking through Sal's jacket as he jogged across the courtyard towards school. He felt uneasy as soon as he pushed open the doors, shaking out his hair so droplets of rain hit the shiny floor of the corridor.

It took him until lunchtime, though, to realize what wasn't quite right: he was attracting attention. Most days, he passed through school totally unnoticed. But today, people kept looking at him. As he tucked into his sad school-issued cheese sandwich, he was fairly certain he saw a girl point at him from the other end of the room.

'Do I have something on my face?' he asked Dirk warily, setting down his sandwich and wiping his sleeve across the back of his mouth.

'Other than oversized eyebrows?' Dirk replied. 'Nope.'

He was busy scrawling a half-hearted history essay, and Sal just rolled his eyes, leaving him to it. Across the table, one of Dirk's other friends was muttering something to the boy next to him. They had their heads bent over a mobile phone, and when they noticed Sal watching them, they grinned as if he were the punchline of a joke.

The mystery wasn't solved until later that day, in English, when Elsie crossed the room and flopped down on to the chair at his side. She dropped her bag on the floor, fixed him with a concerned look and leant in as soon as the teacher's back was turned.

'You all right?' she asked under her breath.

'Yeah,' Sal said.

She raised her eyebrows in disbelief, and it occurred to Sal that if anyone was likely to know what was going on, it was Elsie. She was extremely popular and, therefore, always knew everything about everybody.

He lowered his voice. 'I kind of feel like people are talking about me.'

On the way to class someone had taken the opportunity to yell, 'Ghost boy!' at him in the corridor.

'They are,' Elsie said, looking surprised. 'Didn't you *know*?'

'Know what?'

Elsie pulled her phone from her pocket, tapped away at it for a second, and then handed it to him under the desk.

Sal swore under his breath. She had opened up a regional news website. At the very top of the screen, in bright red letters, were the words: *Our 10 Most Haunted Houses*. Beneath that, there was a photo of his house.

'Did you ask to be featured?' Elsie asked conspiratorially, leaning in to read over his shoulder.

'No,' Sal hissed. His shock fading, he felt a stab of annoyance. 'What would I do that for?'

It wasn't the first time his house had been in the news.

It had been famous before they'd even moved to it, and articles cropped up every now and again when news was thin on the ground. But this was the first one in years – the only one since Sal had been at Holden High. He scanned the paragraph of text underneath the photo.

Located in the idyllic rural town of Holden, this historic house is rumoured to be inhabited by the ghost of a woman abandoned by her husband. She waits, even in death, for his return. Locals steer clear of the place, and the house remains shrouded in mystery.

But if you pass by at night, you may see her shadow in the windows of the attic, where the lights often burn even when nobody is home. It is said the ghosts of her children can be heard too, running up and down the stairs.

'Great,' Sal muttered. He scanned the rest of the list with narrowed eyes.

'House three was home to an axe murderer,' Elsie told him matter-of-factly. She took the phone back out of his hand and scrolled to a picture of a half-ruined cabin surrounded by a barbed-wire fence. 'So it really could be worse.'

Sal felt a sickening sensation settling in his lower stomach. He glanced up and around, wondering who else had seen the article. The room was silent save for the scratch of pens on paper and the muted giggles of two of Elsie's friends behind. Elsie, for once, was not joining in with them.

'I think pretty much the whole school has read it,' she informed him, as if reading his mind.

'Right,' Sal said. 'Of course they have.'

Elsie smiled apologetically and shoved the phone back in her jeans pocket. She pulled out a pack of gum, unwrapped a stick and held it out for him to bite from between her thumb and first finger.

Sal accepted it with his teeth.

Behind them, the giggling got louder, and Sal turned to see Elsie's friends whispering to each other from behind exaggeratedly placed hands. He gritted his teeth and scowled. He had a good scowl, courtesy of his eyebrows, and it usually shut people up.

The girls just giggled harder. One of them bit her lip and winked at him, and he turned back around, flustered.

'Can you ask your friends to stop laughing at me?' he asked Elsie under his breath.

'They're not laughing at you,' Elsie said. 'They're laughing at *me*. And they're not exactly my friends right now.'

Sal frowned. 'What do you mean?'

She shook her head and turned back to face the front of the class, just as the teacher told them off for talking. They spent the rest of the lesson in total silence, save for the snapping of gum and the occasional muted laugh from the girls behind. Sal was so caught up in thinking about the haunted house article that he barely noticed. But when the class ended, he glanced up to see Elsie was looking tearful. Before he could ask her what was wrong, the bell rang and the room became a cacophony of screeching chairs and shouting. Elsie shot him a small smile before gathering her things and sweeping from the room. She was wearing bright yellow Converse that squeaked against the linoleum floors.

'Hey,' Sal called after her, nearly tripping over his own feet in his haste to follow. 'Elsie, wait up!'

He caught up with her in the corridor and rested a hand on her shoulder. She flinched at the contact and spun back around. Her expression melted into one of relief when she saw it was Sal.

'They're idiots,' Sal said. 'Ignore them.'

Elsie and her friends occupied a kind of social high ground that he had never been part of, or had any interest in. But Elsie was sweet, and he felt bad for her.

'They'll have to start talking to me eventually,' Elsie said, shrugging. 'We're all on the winter dance committee together.'

Sal wrinkled his nose up. He couldn't understand why anyone would have any interest in the winter dance, but the event had been the talk of the sixth form since the start of term.

'There's a committee? I thought it wasn't until December?'

'Well, *duh*.' Elsie squinted at him in concern. She tossed her long blonde hair over her shoulder, regaining some of her usual confidence. 'But who do you think plans it? We have meetings every week. I've spent the past month trying to source an ice sculpture within our budget.'

'OK.' Sal was several times more confused than he had

been at the start of their conversation. 'Well . . . um, good luck?'

Elsie laughed, reached out and squeezed his arm before melting away into the crowd. She smiled back at him over her shoulder as she went.

CHAPTER FIVE

Sal kept his head down as he traversed the school corridors, rereading the news article for what felt like the hundredth time. He crossed the courtyard with its dilapidated fountain and pushed through a great wooden door at the opposite end. The sixth-form common room was in the old part of the school, where the original wood panelling still stood strong, though marred by decades of graffiti. Shiny red lockers lined the corridor that led to it, a stark contrast to the arched glass windows and battered wood floors.

There was a brand-new cafeteria, which filled the building with the constant stench of hot grease, and a dusty old library that nobody ever went in, where the books were never arranged in order.

Dirk greeted him on his way to his locker by issuing a

war cry and jumping on his back.

'Did you know about this?' Sal asked him, shaking him off so as to wave his phone under his nose.

'About what?' Dirk asked, busily throwing M&M's into his mouth as they walked. He took the phone and his eyes went comically wide as he read. 'Whoa.'

'Yeah,' Sal said. 'Everyone's seen it, apparently.'

'But this is brilliant!' Dirk said, scrolling excitedly down the article. 'I can't believe no one told *me*. You've not been in the news for ages.'

Sal grabbed the phone back out of his hands and shoved it into his pocket. 'I don't want to be in the news.'

'Well, tough,' Dirk said, slapping him enthusiastically on the back. 'You're practically famous! Look – even that weird new kid is waving at you.'

Sal turned around to see Pax on the other side of the corridor. He was no longer waving. Instead, he was being held up against the lockers with another boy's forearm to his throat, his pale skin flushed nearly the same red as the scarlet lockers behind him. The assailant was a boy Sal recognized from their lunch table. His name was Aiden. He was built like a tank and spoke mostly in grunts.

'What is it?' Sal grumbled. 'National Dickhead Day?'

'You waving at me, freak?' Aiden asked Pax, loudly enough to make everyone in the corridor turn around.

'Nah,' Dirk said to Sal under his breath. He had stopped tossing M&M's into his mouth and was watching the scene unfold with conflicted interest. 'He was definitely waving at *you*.'

Sal groaned in frustration.

'You know him?' Dirk asked.

'Yeah, he's called Pax,' Sal said. *We shared a picnic in a graveyard*, he thought.

'Right,' Dirk said.

They looked back at the scene. Pax's feet had left the floor and were banging against the lockers as he grappled for purchase. He was a good head shorter than the boy holding him.

Dirk was shifting nervously from foot to foot at Sal's side. 'Should I do something?'

'Yes,' Sal said. He passed Dirk his bag. 'Hold this.'

He was already moving, his feet carrying him towards Pax before his brain had caught up. He tapped Aiden on the back and the boy turned, loosening his grip on Pax in order to look at Sal. When he saw who it was, he nodded in gruff recognition.

'All right, ghost boy?'

'Get away from him,' Sal said, his voice tight.

'Why?' Aiden grinned at him wolfishly. 'Whatcha gonna do?'

Something in Sal's head snapped. He felt very light. And then as though his entire body had been flooded with boiling water.

He drew back his fist.

Five minutes later, he was sitting outside the head teacher's office, with Pax across from him practically bouncing up and down in his seat in an effort to catch his eye. The boy was wearing a pair of woolly leggings, fur-lined moccasins and a jumper that reached down over his knees.

It was, essentially, a dress.

Sal was fairly certain it was also the reason they were in this situation in the first place and was therefore finding it intensely irritating. Holden was a small village. People went out of their way to be normal. Especially Sal. Being half-Egyptian set him apart enough already, thanks very much. And then there was the whole haunted house situation. Involvement with Pax was the last thing he needed.

Avoiding the boy's gaze, he studiously examined his own hands. One of his fingers was sticking out strangely and the knuckles of his right hand were turning a vibrant shade of mauve. They were still flecked with blood.

Sal had never broken a nose before, and he hadn't found it to be a particularly pleasant experience. The crumpling of flesh. The crunching of bone. The blood streaming out like water from a tap. All in all, he thought, Aiden had done him a favour by throwing him to the ground. He was pretty sure he would have passed out otherwise.

The combined smell of post-lunchtime chip fat and industrial-grade detergent floating down the corridor was making him feel sick. He closed his eyes, leant his head back on the wall and awaited his punishment.

Holden High's head teacher was a grumpy man called Mr Gulliver who spent a lot of time in his office and the rest of his time with his eyes trained firmly on the ground. He had a large collection of patterned ties and had once tried to solve the school's behavioural problems by playing soft jazz over the speakers during break times.

When he emerged from the office, he blinked like a mole emerging into spring sunlight. His eyes fell on Pax, in all his knitted, woollen glory, and he squinted at him in mild interest before waving him inside.

Sal spent twenty minutes listening to the muted sounds of conversation floating through from the other side of the door. Mr Gulliver seemed to be having trouble getting a word in edgeways. Sal let his eyes drift closed and listened to the excited rise and fall of Pax's voice, too muffled for him to pick out the words.

When Pax was released from the office, he gave Sal an enthusiastic thumbs up and mouthed *good luck* at him as he passed. He was followed by a weary-looking Mr Gulliver, who nodded at Sal and pointed him inside.

The head teacher's office was probably the nicest bit of Holden High. Part of the original building, it was panelled in rich dark wood and lined with cramped, overflowing bookcases. At the back of the room there was a wide desk, overflowing with papers. Squeezed on to one corner was an old-fashioned telephone, and a single highly polished frame holding a photo of a very fat spaniel. At the front of the room were two squashy-looking armchairs and a small round coffee table.

Sal sank into one of the chairs, cradling his damaged fist in his other hand. Mr Gulliver sat opposite him, looked him up and down, sighed heavily and produced a jar of jelly babies from under the coffee table. He removed the lid and slid them towards Sal.

'Pax tells me you saved his life,' he said.

'Bit of an overstatement,' Sal said, choosing a green jelly baby.

'Yes,' Mr Gulliver said. 'I suspected as much.'

When Sal didn't offer any more information, he removed his glasses, polished them and propped them back on the end of his nose. He peered through them at Sal.

'Salem,' he said. 'Salem *Amani*. You must be Asha's brother?'

Adults liked Asha, especially teachers. Sal nodded, hoping this might play in his favour.

It did. Mr Gulliver visibly brightened.

'Lovely girl,' he said. 'Very intelligent. She ran the school paper, of course.'

He gestured across the office at a small selection of trophies that lined one of the bookshelves. There were five in total. Asha had earnt three of them for the school paper while she had been editor. The other two belonged to the chess club and dated back to the 1990s.

'I know,' Sal said. He had been aiming for a polite tone, but the words came out sounding strained. His fist was throbbing painfully.

'Yes, yes . . . I suppose you would.'

Mr Gulliver drifted off into silence again, and Sal wondered if he should be defending himself. It seemed Pax had already done that, though. So he kept quiet in the interest of not making things worse and watched the clock ticking on the wall.

'This is a very inclusive school, Salem,' Mr Gulliver said, after a full minute had passed. He was steepling his fingers together and peering at him over the top of them. 'I don't want you to think I disapprove of your motives.'

'Eh?' Sal said.

'Defending someone you care for is a very noble thing to do,' Mr Gulliver translated for him. He removed his glasses, polished them on the end of his shirt sleeve and then put them back on again, as if to get a better look at Sal's response.

'Um, thanks.' Sal helped himself to another handful of the jelly babies. 'But I don't really know him, to be honest.'

'Heroics aside,' Mr Gulliver said, removing the jelly babies from the table, 'I am still required to suspend you for physical violence.' He gestured at the phone on the desk. 'I've already called home and spoken to your mother.'

Sal stared at him. 'You have?'

'I have.'

'And . . . she agreed with you?' Sal asked, irritated.

Mr Gulliver frowned at him from over the top of his horn-rimmed glasses. 'Why wouldn't she?'

He sent Sal home with only a week's suspension. Sal begrudgingly admitted this was thanks to Pax's deeply flattering version of events, which painted Sal more as a daring vigilante and less as someone who had broken another boy's nose, severely damaged his own hand and nearly fainted at the sight of all the blood.

★

It was one of Asha's days off, and Sal cursed his misfortune when he arrived home to find her sat at the kitchen table, nose in a book, but obviously waiting with bated breath for his arrival.

'Hello,' she said, turning a page with a wry smile.

'Hi,' Sal said, dropping his school bag on the floor. The strap caught on his twisted finger and he swore under his breath.

'So, you're suspended,' Asha said, as if she had been expecting Sal to mess up for some time, and was not at all surprised that it had finally happened.

Sal glared at her. 'Mr Gulliver said he'd spoken to Mum.'

'Oh,' Asha said, smirking. 'Yeah.'

'And?'

'And you're grounded,' Asha said. She pointed to the sprawling mass of Post-it notes that always adorned their fridge. It was their mum's idea of organization. There was a new note in the very centre – its crisp yellow paper wasn't yet curling at the edges. It read *Sal is grounded*.

Sal shrugged. He hadn't been planning on going anywhere anyway. There *wasn't* anywhere to go in Holden.

'What were you fighting over?' Asha asked, giving up the pretence of being interested in her book. She folded down the corner of her page, set it aside and looked at him with a smile that could have rivalled the Cheshire Cat's. 'Was it a girl?'

'No,' Sal said, kicking off his trainers. It was easier, he

thought, not to mention Pax. Sal didn't know why he'd stepped in to protect him, and he certainly didn't feel like explaining it to anyone else. Looking back, the whole situation felt strangely embarrassing. 'It was nothing.'

'So you just thought you'd punch someone?'

Her disbelief was palpable. Sal hadn't ever been much of a fighter. He had once punched a hole in his bedroom wall after an argument with Asha. But until now he had always reserved his aggression for inanimate objects. He hadn't ever hit anyone before. Now that he had, he was pretty sure he wasn't cut out for it.

He pulled his phone from his pocket and loaded the article that Elsie had shown him in English class. He passed it to her. 'Look at this.'

She leant in to examine the screen, shooting him a confused look as she did so. Her expression tightened as she saw the photograph of their house at the top of the article.

'Oh, look,' she said wryly. 'It's us. That's not happened in a while.'

She barely scanned the text before handing the phone back to him.

'Is this what you were fighting over?' she asked. 'You know it's really not worth it.'

Sal rolled his eyes. He turned on the radio to prevent further attempts at conversation, although it was playing a cheesy pop song that made him want to twist his own ears off. He made himself two slices of cheese on toast and retreated to his bedroom to eat them while they were still so hot that the cheddar burnt the roof of his mouth.

He flicked on his television and collapsed on to his bed. A week spent at home lazing around in bed didn't seem like much of a punishment. But he was still left with a niggling sense of injustice which he thought had less to do with his own situation than it did with the memory of the mottled red marks marring Pax's throat.

It was cold in his room and the wind whistled through the window. The floorboards creaked and the paint on the walls was cracking. As he watched, the house groaned in the wind and another crack appeared, running along the length of the wall. He reached up a hand and traced a finger along it.

He tried sketching to take his mind off things, but his hand was still too painful from the punch and he couldn't keep his fingers curled around the pencil. Then he changed into joggers, planning on going for a run, before remembering he was grounded and settling for a round of push-ups on his bedroom floor. Night fell, and he watched *Pulp Fiction* because the static-y hum of his old DVD player always helped him to fall asleep.

When he finally drifted off, he dreamt he and Pax shared a vanilla milkshake and jived on the tables of the high school cafeteria. He woke up in a cold sweat, his heart pounding in his chest.

You remember a time when living in a haunted house felt exciting. Before the darkness within it reached out and grasped you — a cold shock, like the sheets snatched away at dawn. Or an unexpected hand shaking you awake. And you remember, like the first breath of consciousness, the understanding that this, this is not normal. That the life you are living does not neatly fit the checkbox marked reality.

Once the first shock of realization passes, there follows the slow, seeping dread. It curls in the pit of your stomach and thickens in the back of your throat. It clutches deep inside your chest, its fingers threading between your ribs.

The unease is catching. It lies in the bones of the house and spills out like blood into soil, turning warm eyes wary and turning visitors around in their tracks. It is lonely, in this place.

Here, restless days turn into restless nights, until sleep becomes just a memory and blue shadows appear like bruises beneath your eyes.

CHAPTER SIX

Spending a week sitting at home was not as enjoyable as Sal had expected. He was beginning to feel trapped. As the days grew shorter, the house grew darker. Sal started to notice cobwebs he had never seen before, lacing the corners of the ceilings. The rain was incessant, and the smell of rot was setting in. Patches of damp were blooming amid the flowers of the wallpaper.

Within the first few days he had worked his way through an entire box set of Hitchcock films, eaten all of the cereal in the house and taken several dozen naps. He was so bored that he was beginning to wish he would stop waking up from them. At night, he was barely sleeping at all. The house did not fall silent when the sun went down. It was filled with the constant noise of muffled movement. There was a mouse living somewhere in the kitchen below, its scratching impossibly loud in the darkness.

He was having dreams that seemed too vivid, too clear. When he awoke from them, he was left with the uneasy feeling that they hadn't really been dreams at all. Once or twice, head still groggy from sleep, he thought he heard his dad's voice. The sound of his laugh — deep and rumbling. Or him humming, tunefully, under his breath. There had been echoes of him, reverberating in the house, ever since he had died. Sometimes, if Sal left his bedroom window open on warm summer nights, he could still smell cigarette smoke drifting up from the front porch, where his dad used to sit and smoke. He had slept with the window open for months after the accident, until one day his mum had cracked and slammed it closed, causing the glass to splinter in its frame.

On Friday evening he awoke from a fitful sleep to the sound of pans rattling in the kitchen. He was fully dressed and spreadeagled on his bed, where he had been busy staring at the ceiling before dozing off. Outside, the rain had stopped. Sal yawned, scrubbed a hand through his hair and trudged downstairs in the hope of finding some company.

Asha was winding a scarf around her neck. She frowned at him when he appeared in the doorway.

'Where are you going?' he asked, suppressing a yawn.

She gestured at the kitchen table, where the empty casserole dish Sal had hidden at the back of the cupboard now sat. She was annoyed, and Sal could tell because she was smiling at him with narrowed eyes and her lips pursed shut.

'I'm taking that dish back,' she said, picking it up and tucking it under one arm. 'Seeing as you obviously don't want to. It's the cottage by the church, right?'

She was at the front door before Sal caught up with her, tugging on his trainers as he ran. He flung himself between her and the door.

'I'll take it.'

'What?'

Sal pulled the dish out of her hands. 'I'll take the dish back.'

'You can't,' Asha said, looking thoroughly bewildered. 'You're grounded.'

The dish safely in his grasp, Sal smiled at her and strode back down the hall to the kitchen. He pulled the *Sal is grounded* note off the fridge, crumpled it into a ball and held it up for Asha to see. Then he ate it.

He swallowed loudly. 'Not any more.'

Asha stared at him for a full ten seconds before throwing her arms into the air in exasperation. She moved out of the way of the front door. 'You're ridiculous.'

Sal slipped past her out of the house. 'I know.'

It was a perfect autumn night. Crisp and cold and clear. The air was rich with the mingling scents of damp wood, home cooking and rotting leaves. Sal's house was the strangest on Yew Tree Lane. Even at night, the others appeared peaceful rather than creepy. Small stone cottages with thatched roofs and wooden gates. They had potted plants, rather than gargoyles, on their front steps, and warm yellow light streamed out of their windows.

At the very end of the lane was the churchyard. Sal entered over a falling-down stile and wound his way around the graves and through a small thicket of trees that separated them from the cottage beyond. The cottage was made of crumbling grey stone. Flowerpots had been neatly arranged beneath the windows, and there were yellow roses beginning to crawl their way up around the door. Even surrounded by tombstones, Pax's house looked more normal than his own.

Sal hesitated at the gate, stamping his feet against the cold, his breath misting in the air before him. It was silent but for the steady dripping of water from the overhanging trees. He looked down at the casserole dish in his hands, and suddenly felt irrationally and astronomically stupid. Unlatching the gate, he decided to leave it on the front steps and make a hasty retreat.

'Salem?'

He spun around to find a tall, horned figure standing just centimetres behind him. He jumped. So hard that he dropped the casserole dish. It toppled through the air. Then it landed with a crash and shattered into shards on the ground.

'Oh,' the horned figure said. 'Whoops.'

He stepped forward and his face was lit by the warm glow of the cottage windows. It was Pax. He had swapped his usual fur coat for a giant fleecy trench coat, which swallowed him from head to toe. He had paired it with another knitted hat complete with reindeer antlers.

'Was that an accident?' he asked. 'Or did you just really hate the casserole?'

Sal groaned. 'Sorry.' He kicked at the shards with his feet. 'I'll replace it.'

Pax smiled at him and rubbed his gloved hands together, apparently still cold despite having dressed for Narnia. 'We have too many anyway. We needed one for everyone on the lane.'

'Well.' Sal took an awkward step away from the gate to allow the boy to pass. 'I'll see you around.'

Pax's face fell. 'Aren't you coming in?'

'Um . . .'

His hesitation was all the encouragement Pax needed. The boy grabbed his arm and pulled him, with surprising force, through the gate.

'Come on,' he said. 'I have something to show you.'

Sal had only been inside the graveyard cottage once before, long before Pax and his mum had moved in. Back then it had just been a shell of a building. The neighbourhood kids all avoided it — or else dared one another to sneak inside. It had been on one of these dares that Sal had first stepped within its walls. He'd used the window, because the door had been boarded up. The paint on the walls had been peeling. It must've been late autumn because he remembered the sweet scent of overripened apples hanging in the air as he tiptoed over creaking floorboards.

Now, they entered through the front door and the kitchen beyond was warm and cosy. The slate floor no longer crumbled underfoot and the peeling walls had been repainted in a warm shade of terracotta. A bouquet of fiery yellow and orange flowers took pride of place on a scrubbed wooden table. The smell of apples remained, but this time laced with cinnamon and sugar and golden pastry. There was an apple pie on the counter, steaming hot and just pulled from the oven. The house felt as if it had been lived in for years. And, standing by the kettle, there was a woman making tea.

Sal didn't think he'd ever seen a more average-looking person. He glanced at Pax, convinced this overtly ordinary human being could not possibly be family.

'Hey, Mum,' Pax said brightly, wriggling out of his coat.

The woman turned, smiled and did a double take at the sight of Sal standing by her son's side. Her eyes went very wide. Sal shifted uncomfortably in his place. He wondered when Pax had last brought a friend home.

'This is Salem,' Pax told her, unfastening his shoes and apparently oblivious to her astonishment.

'Sal,' Sal corrected.

'Hello,' she finally said, not quite managing to quash the surprise in her voice. She took a sudden step towards him and Sal, for one terrifying second, thought she might be about to hug him. 'I'm Annie. I've heard a lot about you.'

'We're going up to my room,' Pax announced, unfazed.

His mother raised her eyebrows at this and scanned Sal from top to toe, taking in his ripped jeans and tousled hair. It occurred to Sal that he probably looked a little rough.

He hadn't brushed his hair in three days. When her gaze flickered back to Pax, the boy turned pink, grabbed Sal by the arm again and pulled him from the room. He dragged him into a tiny hallway and ushered him up a rickety set of stairs.

'Pax!' The woman followed and shouted up the stairs after them, her voice suddenly gaining an edge of panic.

The boy frowned, not turning around. 'Yes?'

Sal did his best to look non-threatening.

Pax's mother gave them a weak smile, still looking slightly shell-shocked. 'Leave the door open, please.'

Pax's bedroom was in the attic, up two flights of stairs. Entering it from the beige-carpeted, white-walled landing was like entering a different world. The sloping walls were all painted black and strung with fairy lights. A bowl of incense was burning in one corner, filling the room with a sweet, smoky smell. There was a desk surrounded by bookshelves, a bed covered with a tattered patchwork quilt and a cramped little window seat covered with cushions and surrounded by dreamcatchers. The wardrobe was wide open, its contents looking like it would have been better suited to a Womble than a teenage boy.

Sal cleared his throat. 'What did your mum mean? She's heard a lot about me?'

Pax ignored him and launched himself on the bed, throwing his head back on to the pillow. He patted the space next to him expectantly. Sal sat down firmly on the desk chair.

'This is nice,' Pax said, rolling over to stare at him.

On the desk, there was a sandy-coloured hamster in a palatial, multicoloured plastic cage. He was running frantically inside a wheel, little eyes bright and feet a manic whirlwind.

'Oh, look,' Sal said, peering at him. 'It's your spirit animal.'

'That's Aloysius.'

'Allo what?'

Pax giggled as if Sal had said something very funny, and Sal decided to change the subject. He pulled the ends of his hoodie sleeves down over his hands and watched them disappear beneath the threadbare fabric.

'What did you want to show me?'

'Ah, yes.'

Pax jumped up from the bed and crossed the room, leaning over Sal to rummage in a carved wooden box on the desk behind him. When he drew back, he was clutching something in his fist. He pressed it into Sal's hands and flung himself back on to the bed to watch him with satisfaction.

Sal looked down at the object in his hands. It was black and rounded and shiny. He cleared his throat. 'It's a rock.'

'It's *jet*,' Pax said, as if this explained everything.

When Sal continued to look at him blankly, he rolled his eyes and launched into an explanation.

'Well, it has protective properties, doesn't it?' It was obvious from his tone that this was not really a question. 'It dispels negative energy. I read about a case in the *Ghost Hunter's Review*—'

'In the *what*?' Sal interjected.

Pax continued without pause. '—where they used jet to calm an angry ghost in a haunted mansion in Maine.' He pulled a stack of well-thumbed magazines from beneath the desk and returned to the bed to begin leafing through them. 'I'll try and find you the clipping.'

'That's OK,' Sal said. He turned the jet over in his hands. The stone was cool and smooth against his skin. It was, he supposed, a relatively thoughtful gift. And while he wasn't convinced that a pretty piece of rock was going to solve his problems, he was – in that moment – willing to give anything a try. He slipped the stone into his jeans pocket.

'Thanks,' he said, surprised to find that he meant it.

Pax's mother interrupted them, poking her head through the open door and looking relieved to see them sitting at opposite sides of the room. She was carrying a tray with two teacups, a teapot in a floral tea cosy and a plate full of home-made biscuits, which she left on the bedside table. She ruffled Pax's hair fondly before leaving the room.

Sal stood up and examined the room in more detail, tilting his head to read the titles on the boy's bookshelves. He wasn't much of a reader, but he was pretty sure that *The Wind in the Willows* did not belong on the same shelf as *Pride and Prejudice and Zombies*. There were also an alarming number of vampire romance novels, which he politely pretended not to have noticed. He ran his hand along a collection of crystals arranged in front of them.

'Mind the obsidian,' Pax piped up. 'It has a very intense energy.'

'So are you, like, Wiccan or something?' Sal asked nervously. He had found what appeared to be a box of tarot cards on the floor by the bed. He sat down cautiously on the patchwork quilt and opened the box.

'No,' Pax said. 'I just like spooky stuff. It's fun.'

Sal snorted, examining a gruesome illustration of the devil on one of the cards. He helped himself to a biscuit. It was still hot enough to burn his hand, and it melted into a cloud of sweet cinnamon spice in his mouth. 'No, it isn't.'

Pax reached over and took the tarot cards. He arranged two tasselled cushions opposite each other on the bed and scrambled on to one, beginning to shuffle the cards in his hands.

'Sit there,' he said, pointing at the cushion opposite him. 'I'll do you a reading.'

Against his better judgement, Sal did as he was told.

He half expected Pax to lower the lights or put on a spooky voice. But the boy approached the reading with the same level of enthusiasm with which he approached everything else, chatting happily as he shuffled. Sal didn't think he had much of a future as a psychic. Pax eventually pulled three cards from the pile. One by one, he laid them face up on the bed. The Moon, The Lovers and The Three of Swords. Pax leant in to examine them, consulted an instruction booklet for several long minutes and excitedly told Sal that he was going to be unlucky in love.

'Great,' Sal said dryly.

He thought it was probably a good time to leave but it was too much of a relief to have escaped his own house. He settled back against the wall instead and helped himself to another biscuit. Ignoring the card with two people entwined together, he reached out to inspect the one with a picture of the moon. As he reached forward, Pax noticed his sticking-out finger. He reached out and grabbed his wrist. His hands were cold against Sal's, despite the warmth of the room.

'You hurt your hand,' he murmured.

Sal shook him off. He agreed with Asha's assessment of the injury: that it served him right for not making a proper fist. She had subjected him to a lecture on the proper punching technique as soon as she had seen it. 'It's nothing.'

Pax bit his lip. He was still staring at Sal's hand with doe-eyed concern. 'I'm sorry you got suspended.'

'It's not a big deal.'

Pax shook his head. 'Aiden only got a week too. It's not fair. You'll both be back on Monday and it will be like nothing ever happened.'

'Good,' Sal said. 'That's the way it should be.'

Pax fell silent at that. He laced his fingers through the tassels of one of the cushions and stopped meeting Sal's eye.

They sat back against the wall and watched *Psycho* on Pax's laptop, because he had never seen it and Sal could tolerate watching it twice in two days to correct that. They finished the biscuits and Pax turned off the lights so they were lit only by his strings of fairy lights and the glow of the laptop screen.

Not long into the film, Sal fell asleep, lulled by the warmth of the room and the sweet smell of incense. He slept better than he had all week and awoke to the swell of music in the final scene and to find Pax was still watching the film intently at his side. It was gone ten o'clock by the time he left. He apologized to Pax's mother for breaking her casserole dish and she ruffled his hair and told him he was welcome back any time.

Pax leant out of the door to say goodbye to him and Sal ducked his head, feeling awkward.

'See you around,' Pax said.

Sal grinned and backed away down the front path. 'See you around.'

Asha appeared in the living room doorway when he got home, eating tinned mac and cheese out of a pan. She sniffed and then smiled knowingly as he pulled off his trainers.

'You smell like perfume,' she said.

Sal kicked his shoes off. 'It's incense.'

'Oh?' Asha continued to watch him unnervingly.

Sal turned his back on her and took the stairs two at a time. 'Asha?' he called when he reached the top.

'Yes?'

'I broke the casserole dish.'

'You're an idiot,' Asha said.

'Yeah,' Sal said, more to himself than to her. He slipped into his bedroom, closed the door and threw himself on to the bed. 'I know.'

CHAPTER SEVEN

Sal probably shouldn't have been surprised when he opened the door to Pax the very next day. But it was nine a.m., and he was still wearing his pyjamas, and Pax was clutching a large bundle of leaves. So he *was* surprised, and he thought he could probably be forgiven for it.

'Salem,' Pax said, stepping through the front door without waiting to be invited in. 'Good morning.'

He kicked his shoes off, and used his feet to line them up neatly by the door, rearranging Sal's trainers in the process. He peered at Sal over his armful of foliage.

'What are you doing here?' Sal asked, folding his arms. He felt uncomfortably exposed in his baggy sleep shirt and striped pyjama shorts. 'And why have you brought half your garden?'

'It's sage,' Pax said brightly, looking around the hallway

with the same level of interest he had shown when he first set foot inside the house. 'And it's not from my garden. I took it from Mrs Helliwell's.'

Sal grinned reluctantly. Mrs Helliwell was very protective of her garden. As a child, he had once been shouted at for picking a rose over the fence. He glanced warily up the stairs but there was no sign of movement. He thought Asha was probably already awake but, thankfully, she was nowhere to be seen.

Pax tiptoed around the house as if he were walking on hallowed ground. Sal almost expected him to pull out a camera and start taking furtive shots of its details: the twisting carvings on the banisters, the cracks in the walls, the battered antique furniture.

He watched him disappear into the living room before groaning and following suit. Inside, he found Pax already examining his surroundings: toeing at the threadbare Persian rug, peering into the mottled mirror above the fireplace, running his fingers along the spines of the dusty old tomes on the bookcase.

He found a framed photograph of Sal and Asha at primary school, wearing neatly pressed school uniforms and matching grins. Asha's hair was pulled into loose, fluffy pigtails. Her arm was looped around Sal's shoulders. Pax picked the photo up and regarded it with interest. 'You have the same eyes.'

He had left the sage on the coffee table and Sal moved closer to poke at it.

'What are you doing with this?'

Pax produced a box of matches from his back pocket and beamed. 'I'm going to burn it,' he said.

'You're bloody well not,' Sal said, stepping forward and grabbing the box out of his hands. 'You'll set the house on fire.'

'Oh, no.' Pax's eyes widened. 'No, I wouldn't do that. Just a few stems at a time, see?'

He picked one up and wafted it demonstratively under Sal's nose.

'You bundle up a few stems for each room, just enough to make smoke. It's a cleansing ritual that banishes negative forces. You know, for the—'

'Ghosts,' Sal finished for him wearily.

Pax tilted his head to one side and looked at Sal hopefully with very large eyes, vividly reminding him of a puppy begging for treats. His gaze fell to Sal's damaged hand. 'I thought it would be a good way to thank you.'

Sal hesitated, torn between his instinct to get Pax out of the house as quickly as possible and a kamikaze curiosity in what might happen if he didn't.

'Fine,' he said. 'Try it. Just downstairs, though.'

Against his better judgement, he left Pax sitting cross-legged on the carpet with a sprig of sage and the box of matches and stomped upstairs to get dressed. He had pulled on a black-and-grey striped T-shirt and a pair of jeans and was attempting to fix his hair in the mirror when there was a knock at his bedroom door.

It swung open to reveal Asha in the doorway, clutching a takeaway coffee cup the size of her own head and watching him intently through narrowed eyes.

'I don't want to alarm you,' she said. 'But there's a boy performing some kind of ritual in the living room.'

'It's fine,' Sal said. 'I let him in.'

'Strangely enough,' Asha said, 'that doesn't reassure me.'

Sal ignored her in the hope she would leave. He gave up on his hair and began searching for a hoodie that didn't look as if it had been crumpled on his bedroom floor for five days. Asha continued to stand in his doorway, eyeing him in silent assessment.

'He's cute,' she finally said. Then she disappeared.

Weird, Sal thought.

The smell of smoke drew him back downstairs. Pax was wafting a burning piece of sage around in the kitchen with his eyes closed. The leaves were glowing amber and, as Sal watched, one fell to the floor and sizzled out on the tiles.

'Oi,' Sal said. He plucked the sage from Pax's hands and tossed it into the sink. 'That's enough.'

Pax looked disappointed, but allowed himself to be steered into one of the kitchen chairs and offered a cup of coffee. Sal made it decaffeinated, as a form of damage control. Pax added as much milk as he could fit in the mug and, when handed the sugar bowl, stirred in three loaded teaspoons of sugar. By the time he had finished, the drink looked like a milkshake. Sal was pondering the best way to get rid of him when he spoke.

'I really think I should do your bedroom.'

Sal took a large gulp of his own coffee. It was so hot

that it singed his tongue, turning his tastebuds to sand-paper. 'That won't be necessary.'

Two minutes later, he was holding open his bedroom door for Pax, and wondering exactly what had happened.

His room was embarrassingly messy and, compared to Pax's room, incredibly dull. There were a selection of film posters covering one wall and a fist-shaped hole in the plaster by the door. He had a small pile of DVDs by the television and the floor was covered in worn socks and crumpled hoodies, which Sal hurriedly kicked under the bed. There was little in the way of decoration, save for a few Lego minifigures his mother had once bought him and some gifts from Asha: a copper alarm clock, a fancy desk lamp and a sketchbook he had filled with rough pencil sketches. Sal folded his arms defensively as Pax began to slink around the edges of the room. He stopped by the old television and looked through Sal's DVDs as if searching for something.

Sal cleared his throat.

'I still think this is a stupid idea.'

'You said you're not sleeping,' Pax pointed out, un-deterred and still perusing the room. He opened the sketchbook and looked disappointed when Sal whisked it back out of his hands. 'I know it seems a little bit strange—'

'A *little*?'

Pax continued as if he hadn't heard him. '—but I really think it might help.'

Sal threw himself down on the bed and watched with

narrowed eyes as Pax twisted a handful of sage into a neat little bundle.

'So,' Pax said. He removed a length of string from his pocket and wound it around the leaves. 'What do I need to know about these ghosts?'

'You don't,' Sal said.

'It would help to know more about them.'

'Help who?' Sal asked. 'You?'

'Us,' Pax said determinedly.

He sat down next to Sal and helped himself to an ornate brass ashtray from the bedside table. It had once belonged to Sal's father, and he never used it, but he let Pax take it anyway, and watched in unwilling fascination as the boy struck a match and set the feathery tips of the leaves alight. They sizzled and glowed amber, then began to wilt and smoke.

'We don't really talk about it,' Sal said, frowning. He eyed the sage suspiciously. 'In case it makes things worse.'

'Oh?' Pax blinked at him. 'And what if it makes things better?'

Sal flopped on to his back, crossing his hands behind his head. He didn't, for one second, believe that talking about things would make them any better. But neither did he think Pax would let the subject drop without any answers.

'Was it true?' Pax asked. 'What they said in the article?'

'About what?' Sal asked, scowling.

'That they're the ghosts of an abandoned mother and her children,' Pax pressed, unperturbed. 'Do you know who used to live here?'

'No.' Sal shrugged. 'My parents moved in just before Asha was born. It was abandoned for years before that.'

His parents had been enamoured with the house when they bought it. They hadn't cared about the rumours that it was haunted. It had just seemed exciting back then.

'And you have no idea when the problem started?' Pax looked sceptical. 'Or what could be causing it?'

Sal could remember when things in the house had been at their worst. His dad had died when he was just eleven years old. His mum had been convinced that his spirit would join the ghosts that haunted the house. She had barely spoken to Sal and Asha for weeks, sitting motionless in her room, waiting for a sign that he had returned.

'My mum has a theory,' he said. 'That nobody who's lived here ever really dies. Like the house holds on to them, or something.'

'Oh,' Pax said, looking unsure of himself for the first time since Sal had known him. 'But . . . what about your dad?'

'Yeah,' Sal said. 'Him too.'

Pax poked at the burning sage. 'Have you ever—'

Sal cut him off. 'I don't want to talk about it.'

Pax nodded, frowned and bit down on his bottom lip as if to better keep the words in.

They sat and watched the sage smoke in silence, engulfed in the sweet, heavy, earthy scent until it made Sal cough and they had to open a window.

'I think that's enough,' Sal said, tipping the last few

stems out on to the porch below.

When he turned around Pax was examining his DVD collection again. He smiled hopefully at Sal. 'Should we watch another film?'

They watched *The Breakfast Club*, lying on their stomachs on the bed. Pax maintained complete silence for the duration of the film. When it finished, he said he thought it was a shame that they gave the weird girl a makeover at the end.

'She looked better before,' he said, rolling over and stretching like a cat. 'Now she looks exactly like the other one.'

Sal thought he had missed the entire point of the film and told him so.

'It's about fitting in,' he said.

Pax said he thought the point of any film was what you made of it.

'And, actually . . .' he said, 'it's about *not* fitting in.'

He stood up and announced he had to leave, just when Sal had forgotten he was supposed to be getting rid of him. He watched him walk down the drive from his bedroom window and wondered if they had accidentally become friends.

The smell of smoke and sage filled the house for days, and Sal found it oddly comforting. It lingered on his bed sheets even after he'd washed them, and he felt more peaceful than he had in weeks.

CHAPTER EIGHT

'The whole school is talking about you,' Dirk told Sal as they walked through the woods on Monday morning. 'Everyone reckons you're possessed. Oh, and Aiden said he's gonna kill you, but everyone thinks he's a bit of a joke now that they've seen him crying over a nosebleed.'

Sal snorted, wrapping his jacket more tightly around himself. They had taken the shortcut through the woods but the wind was parting the branches around them and whipping icily at their faces. He already attracted more attention than he would have liked to at school, thanks to the rumours that circulated about his house. He didn't want any more.

'I'm amazed people care,' he said.

'Yeah, well,' Dirk said. 'Not much else has been

happening. Apart from Elsie broke up with Jacob because she found out it was *him* that told everyone what happened in the woods. She did it in the middle of the cafeteria and he called her a slut in front of everyone.'

'OK,' Sal said wearily. They hadn't even made it to school yet, and already his head was starting to hurt.

Dirk had been right. The entire school was talking about him. And they continued to do so when he was there, barely bothering to lower their voices. Someone had printed out copies of the *10 Most Haunted Houses* article and pinned them up around the school. Sal removed as many as he could, but soon stopped bothering when they sprang up more quickly than he could tear them down. Year Sevens scuttled out of his way wherever he went. By lunchtime, he was thoroughly fed up of the pointed fingers and the whispering that was following him down the corridors.

He caught up with Dirk in the lunch queue where the boy was piling multiple slices of pizza on to his plate. He was still dressed in his football shorts after PE and was covered up to the knees in mud. There were mud splatters on his face too. Sal thought it was deeply unfair that he was still the one getting all the attention.

'It's a pizza *stack*,' he told Sal excitedly, adding a fifth slice to the tower. 'Tastes better like that.'

'Because there's more of it?'

'Exactly.' Dirk clapped him enthusiastically on the back, oblivious to his bad mood. He added a chocolate milkshake to his tray and shoved another into Sal's hands.

The pizza was swimming in grease, so Sal helped himself to a bowl of congealed pasta instead before following Dirk to their usual table. He glanced up as they approached to see Aiden sitting in the middle of it, laughing along with the rest of the group as he shovelled chips into his mouth. He had a plaster over his nose, but otherwise was the picture of happiness.

'Oh, *c'mon*,' Dirk protested, as Sal made a U-turn and headed for an empty table at the back of the room. 'You can still sit with him, can't you?'

'I literally punched him in the face.'

'So?' Dirk was following him, though reluctantly. 'It's all part of the high school experience. He'll get over it.'

Sal glanced over his shoulder. Aiden had spotted him and his smile had fallen away. He was scowling and pointedly cracking his knuckles. If Sal had less of an instinct for self-preservation, he could quite easily have found it funny.

'I don't think he will.'

'We can't just sit here on our own,' Dirk protested, staring at the empty table as if it might be contaminated. He looked back at his friends.

Sal sat down, and Dirk swore under his breath before slamming his tray down and sitting next to him. He put his earbuds in and refused to speak to Sal for the rest of the lunch break, though he remained firmly in place at his side.

Eventually Sal stole an earphone, and they listened to

The Strokes in a stony silence, arms folded and glaring out at the room. Elsie was reading a book by herself in the corner. Sal assumed this was not by choice, because he had never seen Elsie read a book before, even when they were in English and that was exactly what she was supposed to be doing.

Pax was sitting at the opposite end of the cafeteria, surrounded by his usual circle of empty seats. He was tearing the crusts off a sandwich and gazing dreamily into the distance.

Asha was in the kitchen when he got home from school, tapping away at her laptop, looking unusually cheerful. When she wasn't working, Asha spent all her time on her laptop. Sal had once suspected a secret internet boyfriend, but when he ventured to ask, she had sternly told him that she had no intention of ever falling in love with anybody.

It turned out she was writing. Posts for music blogs; articles for local news sites; and her own personal blog which had gained several thousand followers and which Sal had never quite dared to investigate.

'Hey, Sal,' she said. She snapped the laptop closed as he approached. 'Break any noses today?'

'No,' Sal said. He raised his fist and tapped her gently on the nose with it. 'There's still time, though.'

Asha grinned, pounced and caught him in a headlock, ruffling his hair with such force that he cried out for her to stop.

'It was OK, though?' she asked, once she was suitably

happy that she had inflicted enough pain.

Sal rubbed his head, eyes watering. 'Not really. I've become a social pariah.'

Dirk had been grumpy with him, keeping his earphones in on the walk home. They'd barely spoken since lunchtime, and when they'd parted, they hadn't bothered to say goodbye.

Asha lifted a hand to her heart and beamed at him. 'I'm so proud. Being popular isn't good for you.'

Asha had never had many friends at school, but Sal knew better than to think she had ever really been happy about it. He snorted at her and pushed past, throwing his school bag on the floor and setting off up the stairs.

'Should I order takeaway?' she called after him.

When Sal turned to face her, she was staring up the stairs after him, with furrowed eyebrows. She looked concerned. It was unnerving.

'Yeah,' Sal said, frowning back. 'And stop looking at me like that.'

That night Sal awoke to the sound of phantom noises once more. Dark, vicious voices, and the crashing sound of something fragile splintering. Head still clouded with sleep, he heard the creak of his bedroom door, followed by his mum's voice, tight and anxious.

'Can you hear that, Sal?' she asked. 'You can hear it, can't you?'

He opened his mouth to answer, to tell her that he could, but she had already moved away. There came the sound of something heavy bumping its way down the stairs, and the front door slamming again, followed by the revving of an engine, though when he looked, there was no car on the drive. There was a gale blowing outside and he climbed back into bed, drawing the bed sheets up over his head, curling into a ball beneath them as he waited for the noise to pass.

He reached up to pull the pillow under the sheets and his fingers brushed something smooth and hard.

It was the piece of jet that Pax had given him, tucked safely under the pillow. He had no memory of leaving it there. In fact, he was certain he had left it on the window sill. But the smooth stone felt strangely calming in his grip, and he clenched his fist around it, squeezing his eyes closed and praying that sleep would claim him.

When he next awoke, the house was quiet and early morning sunshine was streaming in through the windows. His fingers were still curled around the jet, and he pushed it back under his pillow before falling once more into sleep.

CHAPTER NINE

Luckily for Sal, Dirk was terrible at keeping his mouth closed. By the morning, he was back to his usual chattering self. Although Sal suspected this may have been thanks to Asha, who had the misfortune of answering the door to him.

When Sal came rushing downstairs, still pulling on his jumper, she was scowling and Dirk was busy telling her she had deep and thoughtful eyes. He was bouncing up and down on the balls of his feet, as close as he could get to Asha without stepping over the threshold. Sal had to manhandle the door closed before Dirk would leave with him.

'We have the same eyes,' Sal said cheerfully, when he had finally got Dirk away from the door and they were walking up the drive together. 'Me and Asha.'

They both had their father's eyes. They were wide-set and the same nearly black shade of brown; identical down to the long, thick eyelashes, which Sal had always found vaguely embarrassing.

Dirk was still riding the afterglow of having spoken to Asha and it took him a while to realize he was being teased.

'What?' he said absent-mindedly, smiling to himself.

Sal batted his eyelashes. 'Are mine deep and thoughtful too?'

Dirk pushed him so hard he skidded two metres down the lane on the rotting leaves and had to break his fall against the trunk of a yew tree. They spent the rest of the walk to school chasing each other through the woods, until they were both gasping for breath and laughing so hard their ribs ached.

At school, the buzz around the online article was still going strong, and Aiden's face was as stormy as ever when Sal passed him in the corridors. Dirk's friends, too, were giving him a wide berth.

When Sal walked into the art classroom that morning Pax was already there. He was curled up in his usual chair by the radiator in the corner. He was knitting.

Sal paused in the doorway and stared dubiously at the giant fluffy creation being crafted in front of his eyes. It was yet to take any real shape, and seemed to simultan-eously require not one, but three balls of bright yellow wool. Pax had lost control of one of them and it was spooling out across the room towards him.

Sal picked it up cautiously and returned it to its owner. He sat down on the nearest free chair and Pax fixed him with a radiant smile, before turning wordlessly back to his knitting, needles clicking furiously. Sal looked on with interest. He had assumed Pax's mother was responsible for his knitted wardrobe. Now, it occurred to him that Pax probably made his own clothes. His bizarre collection of outfits suddenly made much more sense.

Art class was the only time of the school day that didn't make Sal want to simply pack up his backpack and head straight home. There was something soothing about the art classroom, with its wood-panelled walls and wide windows. The rain pattered softly against the panes of glass, but inside was warm and quiet. The tables were battered and worn, and the acrid smell of paint filled the room.

The other students filed in, and the room became a softly buzzing hive of activity. Sal opened his sketchbook and sketched with his arms curved around it, shielding it from anyone else's view. He waited for Pax to start talking at him.

'You ignoring me?' he asked, halfway into the class, when his pencil had begun to hurt his fingers and Pax still hadn't said a word.

He put his pencil between his lips and stretched out his fingers.

'Oh, no,' Pax said, looking astonished. He lowered his knitting needles and turned to fix Sal with his full attention. The yellow wool of his knitting was catching the

77

light streaming in through the windows and Sal suddenly wanted nothing more than to curl up beneath it. 'Of course not. I just thought you might not want to talk to me at school. People don't always.'

Sal remembered the way he had avoided Pax when he'd first started at Holden High. He felt his ears starting to burn and twisted his pencil uncomfortably between his fingers.

'And that's OK,' Pax said, clicking out another few stitches.

'No, it isn't,' Sal said. He lowered his voice. 'Is that why you changed schools mid-term?'

'I enjoy change,' Pax told him, failing to answer his question.

Sal snorted. 'No one *enjoys* change.'

Pax set down his needles and fixed him with an intense stare. Coming from anyone else, the prolonged eye contact might have felt like flirting but, from Pax, it just felt a bit strange. Sal's stomach flipped uncomfortably and he wondered if he was getting sick.

'*I* do,' Pax said.

'OK,' Sal said, for lack of anything better to say. He returned to his sketchbook and added another scribble of shading.

'What are you drawing?' Pax asked, craning his neck in an attempt to see the page. He pulled his chair closer, scraping it loudly against the floor.

Sal sat up straight and tilted the sketchbook away from him. He was drawing a page of crumbling skeletons and was keeping it well shielded in the interests of not looking like a psychopath. 'Just doodling.'

Pax frowned and opened his mouth to question him further.

Sal jumped in before he could speak. 'What are *you* doing?'

Pax shrugged, a smile playing on the corners of his lips. He put on a low grumpy voice, which Sal realized with a reluctant stab of amusement was supposed to be an imitation of his own. 'Just knitting.'

They were interrupted by Ms Henderson, the art teacher, appearing out of nowhere and peering over Sal's head to get a better look at Pax's work. Sal rolled his eyes and edged away, giving her space to sidle in between them.

Ms Henderson liked anybody that did anything different and enjoyed encouraging them all to be *experimental*. Sal stuck to using a pencil and paper most of the time. As a result, she had quickly got bored of him, and he was mostly left to his own devices.

But she obviously adored Pax. She spent the majority of the lesson hovering around him, peering over his shoulder, pointing out whenever he dropped a stitch and occasionally stealing his needles to correct what he was doing.

Sal didn't get another chance to start a conversation. But Pax kept looking back at him, pulling faces at him whenever Ms Henderson intervened. When Sal packed up his sketchbook at the end of the lesson, Pax was still wrestling with his balls of wool.

'Well,' Sal said, pulling his school bag over his shoulder. 'See you at lunch, I guess.'

'OK.' Pax's face lit up as if Sal had suggested a three-course dinner date. 'Yeah. *See you at lunch.*'

Sal sat at an empty table again that lunchtime. Dirk stopped to talk to one of his Year 13 friends on the way past, but followed and sat next to Sal without hesitation.

'Nice to have a bit of peace and quiet,' he said. 'Isn't it?'

Sal didn't think Dirk had *ever* enjoyed *peace and quiet*, or ever would. But he appreciated the gesture all the same. Dirk spent the next ten minutes recounting his goal at that morning's football practice in vivid detail, from the way the ball had hit the back of the net to the bright red burns on his knees where he had fallen to the ground in celebration.

'You should join the team,' Dirk said, for possibly the hundredth time since Sal had known him. 'You're fast, right?'

'Yeah,' Sal said, frowning. 'But I don't like enforced activity. Or teamwork.'

'You're a lone wolf,' Dirk said, nodding.

Things were just beginning to feel normal again when Pax arrived at Sal's shoulder, carrying a tray with two different milkshakes and a bag of cheese-and-onion crisps. He was wearing a feathered poncho and he sat down, uninvited, at Sal's side. Across the table, Dirk snorted with suppressed laughter, then quickly recovered himself under

Pax's unwavering gaze.

'I mean . . . hi?' Dirk offered.

Pax held out a hand for him to shake. There was a selection of thin gold bangles around his narrow wrist that jangled as he moved. 'Pax Delaney.'

'Pax the loony, they call you,' Dirk informed him, shaking his hand.

Sal kicked him under the table.

'Dirk Madden,' Dirk said. 'Pleasure to meet you, Pax.'

Sal sighed, and helped himself to one of the milkshakes. 'Hey, Pax.'

'Hi, Salem.' Pax beamed at him. 'I was going to drink both of those actually, but that's OK.'

He pulled a neatly wrapped peanut butter sandwich out of his bag, which he opened with great care, peeled apart and began to fill with cheese-and-onion crisps. Once he had emptied the packet he turned back to Sal and fixed him with a penetrating gaze.

'I forgot to ask if the smudging helped?' he said.

'The what?' Sal said.

'Burning the sage. It's called smudging.'

Dirk was looking between them, as if watching a deeply confusing tennis match in which both players were breaking the rules. He raised a quizzical eyebrow at Sal, who pretended he hadn't noticed.

'I don't know.' He shrugged. 'No major change.'

'Oh,' Pax said, his face falling.

'But now my bedroom smells like a roast dinner,' Sal said. 'So that's a plus.'

Pax chewed contemplatively on his sandwich. 'There must be something else we can try.' His bracelets jangled as he set it down on the table. 'I'll do some research.'

Sal thought that sounded vaguely alarming. But equally he couldn't think of a way to say so without sounding ungrateful. He settled for staying quiet and hoping that Pax wouldn't come up with anything too outlandish.

'Yo,' Dirk said, drawing their attention back to him. He pointed a chip accusingly across the table at Pax. 'You're really weird. You know that, right?'

'Yes,' Pax said, looking thoroughly unperturbed by the interruption. He picked his sandwich back up and bit into it, crunching loudly.

There followed a very long silence, from which they were eventually distracted by somebody approaching. It was Elsie. She hovered nervously at the side of the table, her long blonde hair half shielding her face.

'Hi,' she said, gaze flitting between the three of them and the empty seats surrounding them. She was smiling but her eyes were red, even beneath the lashings of black eyeliner. She looked hopefully at Pax. 'Can I join?'

'Of course,' Pax effused.

He shook hands with her enthusiastically, bangles clinking, and Dirk pulled a bemused face at Sal across the table. Elsie sat down, smiling properly.

She looked at Sal, with his bruised knuckles and faded denim jacket, and then at Dirk, who had folded his arms across his chest and was back to looking extremely grumpy.

'It's the misfits' table,' she said. She had been carrying a book, which she stuffed back into her school bag, creasing the cover as she did so.

'Speak for yourself,' Dirk muttered.

'Are you being ostracized too, then?' Pax asked, ignoring Dirk and regarding Elsie with intense interest.

'Something like that. None of my friends are speaking to me.'

'They don't sound like friends,' Pax said, through a mouthful of peanut butter.

'No,' Elsie agreed. 'I guess they don't.' She looked Pax up and down appreciatively and reached out to run her fingers over the feathers adorning his shoulders. 'Nice poncho.'

'Mm,' Pax said, his attention back on his sandwich. He licked his fingers clean. 'I know.'

CHAPTER TEN

October stretched on and people began adorning their porches with pumpkins. The days were getting greyer and darker and the local coffee shop started selling pumpkin spice lattes, which were so sickeningly sweet that nobody ever ordered them more than once.

Every night now, Sal was being woken in the early hours by the sounds of movement outside his door. It had become a familiar cycle, one that sometimes skipped and jumped, but always played on a loop like a broken record. It began with the sounds of voices, followed by the sound of something shattering, like breaking china. Then came the thundering of footsteps on the stairs. The heavy thud of something being dragged back down again. The slam of the front door. And the revving of an engine. Finally, the crunching of gravel under spinning wheels, before the whole sequence began all over again. The ghostly voices were the worst of all. The harder Sal tried to ignore them the louder they became.

Before he had even noticed it was happening, he had fallen into the habit of spending all his time at Pax's house. There was something inherently comforting about the tiny little cottage. It was always warm inside and constantly full of the rich, buttery smell of cooking. Pax, it seemed, was perfectly content for Sal to simply turn up and lounge around in his room.

If Sal didn't feel like talking, which was usually the case, he helped himself to one of the books from Pax's shelves and settled himself on the bed, where Pax would chatter away at him without expecting a response. Within a week he had worked his way through the entirety of *A Beginner's Guide to Stargazing* and half of *Wild Ways with Crystals*.

They settled into a routine at school, and Sal realized he liked his new group of friends far more than the old one. They kept to themselves, abandoning their lunch table in favour of hanging out by the radiators in a corner of the library, because Pax was always cold and Elsie always took his side. They talked in hushed voices to avoid the wrath of the librarian and, in return, she let them sneak food inside.

One lunchtime Dirk arrived at their table in the library with a broad grin, looking unusually happy to see them all. He slammed both fists down upon it, causing Pax to jump several centimetres out of his seat and the librarian to shush them loudly. She peered at them over the top of her glasses, looking, as she always did, mildly irritated to see them in there.

'All right, outcasts?' Dirk said in a stage whisper. He pulled out the chair next to Sal's and it screeched against the wooden floor. 'I have a plan.'

'Count me out,' Sal said.

He was drinking watery cafeteria coffee and playing noughts and crosses with Pax, who repeatedly let Sal start and was becoming increasingly confused about why he was losing every time. Elsie was looking on in amusement.

Dirk ignored him. 'My parents are going to visit my nan, so I'm throwing a Halloween party next Saturday. It's exactly what we need. Think of it as a social reawakening.'

He beamed out at them as if expecting them all to break into a spontaneous round of applause.

Sal glowered at him over the top of his paper coffee cup. 'I don't want a social reawakening.'

Elsie cleared her throat. 'Well, *I* wouldn't mind one.'

She missed her old friends, which Sal could not understand. He had seen the way they looked at her in the corridors, and the way they whispered about her behind their hands. He thought maybe she missed her ex too. Sal thought this was an absolute travesty because Jacob, though very popular, was one of the stupidest boys he had ever met.

'See?' Dirk clicked his fingers at her in satisfaction and shot Sal a smug look. 'It'll be great. Everyone who is anyone is going to be there.'

He was interrupted by Pax raising his hand.

'Yes, Pax?'

Pax smiled hopefully, shuffling in his seat. 'Can *I* come?'

Dirk stared back at him in disbelief. '*Yes*, Pax. You can come.'

Sal cleared his throat. 'Do I *have* to come?' In his experience, high school parties always ended with at least one person in tears and at least one more on the floor. He didn't much want to be either.

'You'll love it,' Dirk said, slapping him on the back. 'It's gonna be the party of the century.'

Sal thought that was unlikely.

'Jo's gonna be there,' Dirk continued, as if that might make all the difference. He wiggled his eyebrows suggestively.

Sal had made the mistake of letting Jo corner him under the mistletoe at a Christmas party last year. She was a very tall, very pretty girl with long dark hair and blue eyes. She had also turned out to be an alarmingly enthusiastic kisser and he had been avoiding her ever since.

'Who is Jo?' Pax asked.

'She's the one with the legs,' Dirk told him, as if that answered his question.

'Oh?' Pax raised his eyebrows and rummaged in his school bag. 'I thought they all had legs.'

'Not like that they don't,' Dirk said, going slightly dreamy-eyed at the thought. 'Anyway.' He cleared his throat. 'She's got the hots for Sal. They had a thing.'

'It was a one-off,' Sal clarified, watching Pax dig out yet

another neatly wrapped peanut butter sandwich. His mother had left a bright pink Post-it note on top with a love heart scrawled in biro.

Dirk pulled it off and made a cooing noise, grinning gleefully. He hadn't quite got the hang of not making fun of Pax, but somehow they still got along pretty well. Sal privately thought that this was because Pax found Dirk just as ridiculous as Dirk found him.

On this occasion, though, Pax whipped the note out of his hands and stood up. He swung his bag over his shoulder and stormed away across the library. He was wearing a sort of knitted cape that billowed out behind him, and he cut a surprisingly majestic silhouette as he went.

Dirk whistled quietly, looking shell-shocked. 'What's his problem?'

'You're an arsehole?' Elsie suggested.

Sal watched Pax disappear through the library doors, fighting the urge to follow him.

Exactly how Sal had ended up becoming friends with a group of extroverts was entirely beyond him. He spent the days leading up to the party sulking while the others happily planned costumes, playlists and decorations.

'I still think it's a bad idea,' he told Dirk on the Tuesday before the party.

It was half-term, and pouring with rain. They were all holed up in Dirk's living room. His family's Labrador, Grey, had fallen in love with Pax the second he'd walked in the door, and the two were curled up on the sofa together. Dirk and Elsie were sat on the carpet, playing an increasingly aggressive game of *Mario Kart*, eyes fixed on the TV screen.

'It's a great idea,' Dirk said, thumbs darting over the controller. He glanced over at Sal. 'And you've gotta bring Asha too, mate. I think I'm getting somewhere with her.'

'I'm pretty sure you're not,' Sal said.

Dirk's kart hit a banana skin and crashed off the course. He swore, throwing the controller over his head, forcing Pax to duck as it flew over the top of the sofa. Elsie crossed the finishing line and whooped in victory.

'How long have you liked Asha?' she asked, setting her controller aside and lying back on the carpet in self-satisfied contentment.

'For ever,' Dirk said emphatically. 'We were in the same class at primary school. But she got moved up a year, 'cause she's so smart.'

'So you're the same age?' Elsie asked. 'I thought she was older.'

'She is,' Dirk said. 'But not by much.'

'She's eighteen next month,' Sal said. He was scrolling on his phone, already bored of the conversation.

'So she's a Scorpio,' Pax said, with an air of great significance.

'Yeah,' Dirk said, absent-mindedly. 'Virgo rising.'

Sal put down his phone and stared at him.

'What?' Dirk disappeared behind the sofa to retrieve the controller, avoiding Sal's eye. 'My mum's big into astrology. She's got all the magazines and stuff.'

89

When Sal got home that afternoon there was a man on the front lawn, holding a camera and staring up at the house. This was unusual. What was even more unusual was that Asha was standing next to him. And the two appeared to be deep in conversation.

Sal climbed the gate at the end of the drive with care, hopping down lightly so as to not make a noise when he landed on the gravel. Neither Asha nor the stranger noticed as he approached, and he was nearly close enough to hear what they were saying when he slipped on a patch of wet grass and went down with a bump.

'Hi, Sal,' Asha said, without turning around.

'Hi,' Sal said, standing up and brushing gravel off his scratched and reddened palms.

The stranger had turned to face him. He was wearing a grey suit jacket over a retro *Ghostbusters* T-shirt and a pair of jeans. Sal took an instant dislike to him, with his scruffy hair and hipster clothes. He wondered if the *Ghostbusters* T-shirt was supposed to be ironic.

'Who's this?' Sal asked, addressing Asha.

'Faris Jones, *Holden Herald*,' the man said, before she could respond. He held out a hand for Sal to shake, failing to hide the eagerness in his voice.

Sal stared at it until he lowered it, unshaken.

'I'm hoping to write an article on your house. I read the *10 Most Haunted Houses* feature online.' He grinned. 'Seemed like too good an opportunity to miss.'

'Right, well . . .' Sal said. 'Unlucky.'

The reporter removed a notebook from his back pocket and consulted it with a furrowed brow. 'You must be . . . *Salem*.'

'Sal,' Sal corrected. 'You need to leave.'

'*Sal*,' Asha protested, looking horrified by his rudeness.

The man pursed his lips and returned the notepad to his pocket. 'It's nothing to worry about, kid. Just a short article for a little local colour.'

Asha smiled at the man apologetically. 'You probably *should* get going.'

Sal didn't miss the flash of disappointment in the reporter's eyes. Although it was hastily concealed with a smile. He rummaged in his pockets and pulled out a business card, passing it to Asha before he turned to leave.

'Call me any time,' he said.

Sal watched him trudge away down the driveway with narrowed eyes. When he turned back to interrogate Asha, she was already at the front door, kicking her shoes off and looking nonchalant.

'What's going on?' he asked, catching up with her and closing the front door behind them.

Asha sighed. 'Nothing. He wants to write an article, like he said.'

'Well, did you tell him not to?' Sal asked, frowning.

'No point,' Asha said. 'They'll write what they want.'

A horrible thought occurred to Sal. 'You weren't giving him an interview, were you?'

Asha laughed outright at that. 'Don't be ridiculous, Salem. We're not the Kardashians.'

Embarrassed, Sal reopened the door a crack and peered out to watch Faris Jones disappearing over the gate and down the lane. 'I just don't think it's a good idea to talk to them.'

But Asha, as usual, wasn't listening. Instead, she turned and disappeared up the stairs, obviously deep in thought. Quashing his unease, Sal shook his head and let her go. Asha wasn't somebody who could easily be reasoned with. She always believed, with unshakeable conviction, that she knew best.

CHAPTER ELEVEN

'Why did we agree to this?' Dirk asked Sal as they trudged through the pumpkin patch.

It was the morning of the Halloween party and Elsie and Pax had ganged up to insist that they carve pumpkins. It was crisp and cold and the ground crunched beneath their feet. The field was filled with the ripe, earthy smell of pumpkin and the oppressive stench of manure from the nearby farm. Pax and Elsie had disappeared into the distance, his gloved hand clasped in hers, as they leant down to take stock of their options.

Sal wasn't sure when it had happened, but the two of them had started sharing wardrobes. Elsie had turned up in Pax's feathered poncho, which Sal found more than a little disconcerting. She was wearing plaits in her hair and golden eyeshadow and looked like Pax's long-lost sister.

Dirk was watching them leap across the field, jumping pumpkins and laughing. He frowned.

'Are they a thing now?' he asked.

'Eh?' Sal followed his gaze. 'No. I think Pax is gay.'

Dirk's eyes lit up as if Sal had told him something especially juicy and exciting. 'Why?'

'He reads these vampire romance novels,' Sal said.

'Like *Twilight*?'

'Like *Twilight*, but with less sulking and more boys kissing.'

'Whoa,' Dirk said. He squinted across the field at Pax, looking strangely impressed. 'No way.'

'Don't go round telling people, though,' Sal said. He suddenly wished he hadn't said anything. He didn't know if Pax was out or not. He thought Pax's mother knew, but it wasn't clear whether that was the result of an actual conversation or just Pax's affinity for romance novels and scented candles.

Dirk was a good listener. But he was a better talker, and he was terrible at keeping secrets. He nodded, though, looking unusually serious, and mimed zipping his lips together.

'I bet he's into me,' he said confidently, ruffling a hand through the jet-black coils of his hair. He was wearing football shorts despite the chill, because he liked to show off his legs.

'Dirk, mate?' Sal said.

'Yeah?'

'*No one* is into you.'

They chose a pumpkin each and stopped at the farm shop cafe, a tiny wooden building that had once been a barn and was now filled with rickety tables and chairs. Elsie's older brother was working as a waiter and happily turned a blind eye to their age, serving them hot mulled cider and a free stack of French toast when his manager wasn't looking.

'Are these your new friends?' he asked Elsie, grinning broadly, eyes flickering around the table in obvious fascination. His eyes lingered on Pax, as everybody's always did. He was wearing his fleecy trench coat and was still holding his pumpkin in his lap, apparently reluctant to leave it under the table with the others.

Elsie took a piece of French toast and bit into it viciously. 'Go away, Michael.'

Michael nodded, and mimed wiping the smile off his face. 'OK.'

Once he'd reached the other end of the cafe, he called over his shoulder, 'ELSIE?'

'*What*?' she hissed, teeth clenched, as half the people in the room turned to look at her.

'I like them better than the last ones,' he yelled.

'We *are* better than them,' Dirk agreed, making Elsie turn on him with a withering glare.

They left the farm carrying their pumpkins, and by the time they arrived at Dirk's house, their arms were aching. All apart from Pax, who had chosen a small yellow pumpkin because he said he felt sorry for it.

Dirk lived on what Sal liked to think of as the *sensible side* of the village. The houses were newly built, and not encircled by ancient trees that blocked out the sunlight. There were no graveyard cottages or hulking haunted houses. There was just row upon row of neat red-bricked buildings, with symmetrical windows and shiny white front doors.

The four of them traipsed into the house, pink-cheeked from the cold and leaving muddy footprints in their wake. Dirk's parents had only left for his nan's house the day before, but the kitchen was already showing signs of neglect. There was a pile of dishes in the sink, crumbs covering the floor and a forgotten slice of pizza withering away in a grease-stained box on the countertop. They crowded around the table, armed with a selection of knives, and set to work.

'I don't know why we're bothering,' Dirk said, ten minutes in. He was wrestling the top off his pumpkin, amid a shower of seeds. 'Someone's just gonna throw up in one of them.'

Elsie shot him a dark look and stabbed out a nose for her own pumpkin. She was using a kitchen knife the length of her own arm. 'You can't have a Halloween party without decorations.'

Pumpkin carving with Elsie wasn't much fun. She had been in a bad mood since they'd met her brother at the farm, and the scowl had become etched into her face. She was carving a matching one into her pumpkin, wielding the knife with alarming precision.

Sal didn't think she had taken kindly to being embarrassed.

'Who gave the grumpy girl a knife?' he asked, when she stabbed it into her pumpkin with such force that the table shook.

Elsie clicked her tongue. 'Who gave the angry boy a knife?'

Sal laughed. 'I'm not angry.'

'Is he angry?' Elsie asked the room at large, as if consulting a jury.

'You're a bit angry,' Dirk said. He caught Sal glaring at him and averted his eyes. 'Sometimes.'

Sal looked over at Pax for support, but he appeared to have conveniently stopped paying attention. He was elbow-deep in pumpkin innards as he pulled handful after handful of seeds out on to the table, bottom lip caught between his teeth in concentration.

When they had finished carving, they lined the pumpkins up on the table to compare. Pax's pumpkin was smiling. Sal had given his own pumpkin a wide, screaming mouth. It was staring at him with round, hollow eyes. Elsie and Dirk had both carved long jagged grins and triangular eyes and were busy arguing about whose was better looking.

'It's a shame we can't have the party at Sal's,' Elsie said, once she had won the argument. She turned to him accusingly. 'Your house is dead creepy.'

'*My* house is creepy?' Sal grumbled. 'Pax *literally* lives in a graveyard.'

'Yeah, but your house is haunted,' Dirk said, flicking a pumpkin seed across the table at him.

'There was a reporter sniffing around the other day,' Sal told them. 'Said he's writing an article. I think he was trying to interview Asha.'

'Neat.' Dirk's eyes lit up. 'She should do it, man. You could be famous.'

Sal snorted. 'Yeah – famously weird.'

'What kind of an article?' Elsie asked, looking concerned. 'Saying what?'

'I don't know,' Sal said. He stared down into the hollow eyes of his pumpkin. 'I just wish I lived somewhere else.'

Pax was looking thoughtful. He rested a pumpkin-covered hand on Sal's arm. It was stained orange and somewhat slimy but, somehow, still soothing.

'Maybe we should try lavender?' he said, patting Sal's bicep in what he obviously thought was a reassuring manner. 'It has a calming influence.'

'Pax,' Sal said, unable to hold back a smile. He slung an arm around his slender shoulders and squeezed. 'I don't think lavender is gonna cut it.'

They didn't part ways until the afternoon, when they had finished draping the house in cobwebs and the sun had begun to set. Elsie waved goodbye and disappeared towards the centre of the village while Pax skipped along at Sal's side on their way back to Yew Tree Lane.

CHAPTER TWELVE

It was a cold night. The day lost the golden sheen of autumn when the sun dipped below the horizon and a bleak mid-winter darkness had descended. When Asha arrived home from work, she had a bottle of vodka for Sal, which she handed to him with a grin and told him not to drink all at once. Her boss at work had insisted they all dressed up for Halloween, and she had woven gold ribbon into her braids and applied lashings of black winged eyeliner.

'Weren't you Cleopatra last year too?' Sal asked.

'Yes,' Asha said, voice dripping with impatience. 'But I'm pretty sure I was also Cleopatra in a past life, so it's only fair that I get dibs on the costume.'

She had written her university admissions essay on Cleopatra. Sal remembered her sitting hunched over her laptop at the kitchen table, pounding at the keys with alarming enthusiasm. When he had asked what she was writing about, she told him it was about why women were natural leaders who didn't need men. Then she had asked him to make her a cup of tea.

'Are you coming to the party?' Sal asked, remembering Dirk's instruction to bring her.

'God, no,' she said, then disappeared up the stairs and into her room.

She was lying on her bed tapping away at her laptop by the time Sal had worked up the courage to follow her. He hovered cautiously in the doorway until she noticed him. She looked up and raised an eyebrow and Sal considered retreating. Cleopatra raising an eyebrow at you was a pretty intimidating sight.

'The thing is,' he said hesitantly, 'Dirk really wants you to come.'

Asha went right back to typing. 'Believe it or not, Salem, my life does not revolve around what boys want from me.'

Sal didn't really have an answer to that. He nodded and retreated from the room, closing the door behind him.

At eight o'clock exactly, Pax arrived at the front door draped in a long white sheet. The only parts of him visible were his giant grey eyes, which seemed to smile at Sal through the holes cut into his costume.

Sal shook his head. 'Seriously?'

'I thought it was appropriate,' Pax said, his voice

muffled by the fabric covering him. He gestured around the hallway, as if he thought he was now suitably dressed to be inside. 'What are you supposed to be?'

Sal shrugged. He was wearing a faded The Clash T-shirt that had once belonged to his father, a battered leather jacket and a pair of black jeans. He had tried to make his hair look somewhere approaching stylish but it had ended up looking the same as it always did: messy.

'Myself?' he said.

'That's scary enough,' Asha said behind him. She was standing on her tiptoes so as to get a better look at Pax over his shoulder.

Pax was still staring critically at Sal. He pulled off his sheet and folded it over one arm before turning to Asha. 'Can I borrow your eyeliner?'

Sal grudgingly followed the two of them upstairs and into Asha's bedroom. Her room was smaller and much tidier than Sal's. She had wanted to be a journalist for as long as Sal could remember, and the walls above her desk were plastered with clippings of her articles from when she had been editor of the school newspaper.

It had been years since he'd last read them, and he was scanning them with mild interest when a pair of hands landed on his shoulders. He was forcibly pushed on to Asha's bed and attacked with an eyeliner pencil.

Pax leant over him, resting one hand on his chin while he applied eyeliner with the other and repeatedly telling Sal off for blinking. He was wearing a white T-shirt and faded jeans. It was the plainest outfit Sal had ever seen him in. He smelt good, like freshly baked cookies and washing powder, and Sal was too busy inhaling to argue with him. Across the room, Asha was reclined in her desk chair with her feet up on the desk, watching them with obvious fascination.

'You're a punk,' Pax declared, when he had finished.

Asha found them a handful of safety pins and Pax pressed them carefully through the leather of his jacket, his hand on the inside to prevent them piercing Sal's skin. His tongue was poking out in concentration. When he had finished, he took a step back and looked him up and down appraisingly.

'You look good,' he said. Then he pulled his sheet back on over his head.

On his way out of the room, Sal paused to assess himself in the mirror. The eyeliner made his dark eyes even darker, but somehow made him look thoughtful rather than grumpy. He didn't hate it. He frowned, rumpled his hair and stared, disconcerted, at his own reflection.

'I used to be normal before I met you,' he told Pax.

Asha made a doubtful noise in the back of her throat.

Pax just laughed. 'There's no such thing.'

Asha followed them to the top of the stairs and watched them go. 'Will you be late?' she called after them, as they reached the front door.

'It's a party, Asha,' Sal said. 'I'm gonna be late.'

'Oh,' Pax said. He withdrew a messy twisted wreath of silvery green stems and purple flowers from somewhere under the folds of his sheet and hung it neatly on the coat hooks by the door. 'I nearly forgot.'

Asha looked baffled.

'Lavender,' he said. 'For protection.'

Sal steered him out of the door before his sister could respond. She was already on her way down the stairs to examine the wreath.

'Bye, Asha,' Pax called over his shoulder.

'Bye, Pax,' she shouted after them, voice rich with amusement. And then, at the top of her voice, with more bite: 'Bye, Salem.'

CHAPTER THIRTEEN

Sal and Pax took the shortcut through the cornfield to get to the party, crunching fallen husks beneath their feet, and using the lights from their phones to guide the way. The field was dotted with rabbits. They scattered as they approached, diving out of the white glow.

Pax was unusually quiet as they walked, and when Sal asked why, he turned to frown at him.

'Why didn't you tell me I'd been saying your name wrong?' he asked. For the first time since Sal had known him, he sounded unhappy.

'I did,' Sal said. 'It's Sal.'

'No,' Pax protested. 'Your full name. Salem. I've been pronouncing it wrong.'

'Everyone does,' Sal said. 'Anyway. I don't care. I like it the way you say it.'

He had always been Sal, because Salem never really fitted him, no matter how it was pronounced. But he really had grown to like the way Pax said it. Sure, technically it was wrong, but he always sounded like he was enjoying using it.

Pax cocked his head and narrowed his eyes. 'Really?'

'Really.'

That appeared to cheer Pax up. And, after a few more minutes of quiet, he seemed to forget his annoyance and began his usual onslaught of chatter. When he said Salem's name again, though, he pronounced it correctly and glared at him, as if daring him to comment. Sal grinned down at the ground, refusing to meet his eye.

They heard the party before they saw it: the pounding music and the yells of teenagers. Dirk had invited half of the school, and it looked like the other half had turned up anyway. People were overflowing from the front door, spilling out into the garden, which they had draped with fake cobwebs and lit with the carved pumpkins.

Inside, the house was dark, every room heaving with people shouting over the pounding of the music. Everyone had dressed up, and Sal found himself repeatedly getting tangled in other people's costumes as they moved through the house searching for Elsie and Dirk. Pax was hanging on to the back of his jacket to avoid losing him in the crowd.

They found them both in the kitchen. Elsie had dressed as a witch, complete with a silver-and-green striped scarf and shiny buckled shoes. She was drinking something out of a cauldron with a twisty straw. A group of her old friends were laughing together in the opposite corner, but Elsie was studiously ignoring them and waved Sal and Pax over as soon as they walked in.

Dirk was half wrapped in toilet paper in a lacklustre attempt at dressing as a mummy. He was already very drunk and only wanted to talk about one thing: Asha.

Why wasn't she with them? Was she coming later? Had she dressed up?

When Pax told him she had dressed as Cleopatra for work, he let out a tortured groan.

'Well,' he said, brandishing his can of cider and splashing them both with Strongbow. 'It makes sense. The girl *is* a goddess.'

Sal grimaced and went to pour himself a vodka and coke. The kitchen table was covered in sticky glass bottles, half of them already empty.

'Cleopatra was a queen, actually,' Pax was saying behind him. 'Not a goddess.'

Dirk wasn't listening. He had spotted a group of football friends at the other side of the room and was bouncing off towards them, shouting as he went.

'He's right, though,' Pax said. 'Asha's really nice.'

Sal pulled a face. 'You don't have to live with her.'

Sal thought the last time Pax had been to a party had probably been when there was still jelly and ice cream on offer. He had brought a two-litre bottle of lemonade with him and didn't seem to have any interest in mixing it.

In his ghost costume, it was nearly impossible for

anyone to tell who he was, and he was making the most of this by holding conversations with everybody in the room. Floating from one group to the next with ease, leaving people smiling in his wake. Sal drew the line when he caught sight of him joking with Aiden, who was nearly doubled over with laughter and obviously completely unaware of who he was talking to.

'C'mon,' he said, grabbing Pax by the arm and pulling him away.

'Hey,' Pax complained, as he allowed himself to be dragged to the other side of the room. His eyes sparkled at Sal from underneath his sheet. 'I was socializing.'

All around them, people were dancing to the thrumming beat of 'Ballroom Blitz'. More people kept piling in through the front door. The living room was full of drunk people, who pushed past them, jostling them against each other.

'You shouldn't have to disappear,' Sal said, plucking at his ghost sheet, 'to make people like you.'

Pax met his eye and stared at him unnervingly.

Sal looked away. 'I'm getting another drink.'

Sal's head was spinning. Someone was passing him his third or fourth or fifth drink. Pax had thrown off his sheet and was dancing alone in the centre of the room, swaying to the beat. There was a halo of empty space around him, despite the crowd. He hadn't had a sip of alcohol but he still danced like the drunkest person in the room. His eyes met Sal's and his face seemed to light up in the semi–darkness, his blond hair shining in the orange glow.

Jo was there, as Dirk had promised. She was dressed as a cat in pointy ears and a tight leotard that showed off her long legs. She looked beautiful and she kept trying to talk to him, but Sal kept forgetting to listen, too busy laughing at Pax to hear what she was saying. Several minutes into the conversation, he realized he hadn't replied in a while and looked round to see she had disappeared and he was standing on his own again in the corner of the room.

Then he was sitting on the sofa and Pax was perching on the back of it with his legs slung over Sal's shoulders, leaning down to talk incessantly into his ear. It was quieter and the crowd had thinned. Dirk was kissing Jo in the corner and Sal was feeling irrationally indignant on Asha's behalf. The entire house was full of the smell of cigarette smoke and cheap beer. Pax was messing up his hair, his long fingers carding through it, trying to pull it into spikes. Sal was batting him away. Elsie was laughing at them from across the room.

They left at two a.m., when Sal could no longer stand up without the room spinning. Elsie was asleep on the sofa and Dirk had disappeared upstairs with Jo. When they stepped outside, the sky was completely clear of clouds and the night air was so bitterly cold that it stung when it hit Sal's face. At some point during the night Pax had tied his sheet around his neck, and he was trailing it along behind him like a cape. For once, he didn't seem to be feeling the cold.

Pax pointed at the stars and told him to look up. Sal got

lost in the constellations, the ground swaying beneath his feet. When he looked back at Pax, the boy was laughing and running away from him down the street.

Sal followed him, his feet pounding on the pavement, which felt like it was tilting and tipping beneath him. The street lights flashed by in streaks of golden light and with the wind on his face he felt like he was flying. He shouted Pax's name, gaining on him, reaching out to grab him when the boy jumped over the stile and into the cornfield. He disappeared amid the shadowy stems and Sal plunged after him. The ground crunched beneath his feet and the corn cracked as he raced through it.

Pax's sheet was billowing out behind him, bright enough for Sal to see in the moonlight. He chased him until his heart was pounding, and his ears were burning with cold. Pax was slowing down and turning around, raising his hands in surrender as he backed away, laughing, down the path. Sal drew to a stop and launched himself at him, tackling him to the floor and straddling his waist. He grabbed him by the wrists and held them high above his head, pressing them down into the ground as he grinned in victory.

Pax was laughing and squirming beneath him, still gasping for breath. Time passed and Sal didn't move. Then Pax wasn't laughing and was just staring up at him, lips parted and eyes wide.

Sal's entire world tilted. He rolled off him, scrambled to the side of the path and vomited into the cornfield.

CHAPTER FOURTEEN

W hen Sal woke the next morning, it was to the warmth of his own bed and a pair of big grey eyes blinking down at him. Pax was dressed in one of Sal's hoodies and smelt strongly of his black-pepper-scented shower gel. His hair was damp and curling. He was smiling, head tilted to one side, as he held out a cup of coffee.

Sal jerked upright so quickly he nearly headbutted him.

'Good morning,' Pax said serenely, holding the mug out to him with both hands.

Sal accepted the cup, stared into the inky depths and wondered when Pax had noticed he liked his coffee black. The boy jumped on to the end of the bed and beamed at him. Sal's hoodie was too big for him and he'd rolled the sleeves to his elbows, making his forearms look pale and slender.

'You're still here,' Sal pointed out. His head was pounding and he was still dressed in last night's clothes. One of the safety pins in his jacket was digging uncomfortably into his ribs. His mouth tasted like something had died inside. He hurriedly wiped his chin on his sleeve, fairly certain he had been drooling in his sleep.

'I slept on the floor,' Pax said. He nodded at a sort of nest he had fashioned from an old blanket, a selection of cushions and one of Sal's own pillows. 'I didn't want you to choke on your own vomit.'

Sal swallowed his embarrassment with a mouthful of coffee. 'Sorry.'

He had only a vague memory of getting home the night before, of being tugged up the stairs and carefully manhandled into his own bedroom.

Pax looked confused. He drew his knees up to his chest. 'Why? I had fun.'

'Right,' Sal said, closing his eyes and biting back a grin. 'Of course you did.'

He yawned, and stretched his arms out over his head, to discover the lavender wreath Pax had given him was now encircled around his wrist.

'Can you not *decorate* me in the night, please?' he asked grumpily.

'Oh,' Pax said, looking thoroughly unconcerned. 'No. That wasn't me. You must have done it yourself.'

Sal didn't know what might have possessed him to do such a thing. But neither did he think Pax was lying. He looked back down at the lavender wreath, pulled it off and frisbeed it across the room. Goosebumps had risen along the length of his arms, but he put it down to the chill and pulled his sleeves to his fingers.

Pax's phone rang. He winced at the sound of it and hurriedly dug it out of his pocket, cutting off the caller before sending a text.

'Is that your mum?' Sal asked. He was remembering the way Pax's mother had looked him up and down when they'd met. And her expression of alarm when she'd seen them disappearing into Pax's bedroom. 'Won't she mind you staying over?'

Pax ignored the question. His phone chimed again, and he stabbed out a response with one finger. His tongue poked out as he typed. Sal got the impression he didn't use his phone very often. When he had finished, he slipped it back into his pocket and smiled up at Sal.

'You're more like me when you're drunk,' he said, resting his chin on his hands and staring at him intensely.

'Pax?' Sal said.

'Yes?'

'*Everybody* is more like you when they're drunk.'

Sal took a hurried shower to make himself feel more human, relishing the hot water as it beat down on his skin, drowning out the throbbing in his head. When he got back to his bedroom, fully dressed and running a towel through his hair, Pax had disappeared. Sal found him in the hallway, carefully hanging the lavender wreath back on the coat hooks by the front door.

His eyes lit up as Sal approached, and he announced he was hungry with such an air of expectation that Sal found himself making breakfast, even though he never ate it himself. His own stomach was churning and he was beginning to wish that he too had stuck to drinking lemonade.

'I was awake half the night,' Pax told him, 'listening for ghosts.'

'Did you hear anything?' Sal asked.

'Nope,' Pax said, looking deeply disappointed about it. 'I did think I saw one, though. It was bright blue, and sort of *glowy* looking.'

Sal squinted at him in confusion. He'd never seen anything of the sort.

'But then I woke up,' Pax finished lamely. 'I think I was dreaming.'

Sal made him toast slathered with chocolate spread, and a coffee so milky he couldn't help wincing in disgust when he handed it to him. Pax spooned three heaped teaspoons of sugar into the mug and Sal had to avert his gaze.

They were still in the kitchen, drinking more coffee, when Asha arrived, rubbing sleep out of her eyes and wrapped in an old tartan dressing gown and big white bunny slippers. Her braids were piled into a wild, messy arrangement on top of her head.

'Oh,' she said, stopping abruptly in the doorway and looking suddenly unsure if she should enter. Her gaze flitted from Sal to Pax and back again. 'Hi, Pax.'

'Hi,' Pax said happily. He gestured at her slippers. 'They look cosy.'

Asha took that as permission to enter. She fixed Sal with a questioning expression as she passed him and he shrugged in return.

'Is your mum in?' Pax asked Sal. He was looking hopefully towards the hallway. 'Can I meet her?'

'Bit soon to meet the parents, isn't it?' Asha asked. She padded across the kitchen and began rummaging in the cupboard for cereal.

Sal ignored her. 'She'll still be asleep,' he told Pax. 'She works weird hours.'

Pax's phone was continuing to chime every ten seconds, but he was no longer answering. Sal was pretty confident it was Pax's mother, sending a string of furious texts. His suspicions were confirmed when the house phone rang. Asha answered, listened for a moment and passed it wordlessly to Pax, who turned pink and disappeared into the hall with it.

He needn't have bothered. Sal and Asha could hear the woman shouting down the line from where they sat at the kitchen table. Asha cast Sal a disapproving look, which he ignored, slurping down the dregs of his coffee.

'Well,' Pax announced, arriving back in the kitchen, carrying the phone as if it might explode in his hands. He passed it to Asha and brushed toast crumbs off the hoodie he had stolen from Sal's wardrobe. 'I should get home. I promised Mum I'd help with the Sunday baking.'

Sal grimaced. He didn't think sending Pax home at

114

nine in the morning, wearing his clothes and smelling of his shower gel, was the best way to convince the boy's mother they weren't dating. It probably wasn't a good way to stay on her good side either. On the other hand, it seemed a bit too late to do anything about it.

He walked him to the door and Pax flung his arms around him in a brief, somewhat suffocating hug before darting out of the door and down the drive.

Asha cleared her throat behind Sal. She was wearing the same expression she adopted when she was about to start lecturing Sal on whose turn it was to do the hoovering (it was always his). He tried to move past her, but she stood her ground, folding her arms across her chest.

'I don't think he should be staying over,' she said.

'He's not. It was a one-off.'

Asha raised both eyebrows and smirked.

'Not like that,' Sal snapped. 'We're *friends*.'

Asha sighed, her smile disappearing. She scrubbed a hand across her face, as if she was the one with the headache.

'You know we can't have people round at the moment.'

Sal's eyes fell on the lavender wreath on the hooks up by the front door. On the hallway table beneath it, next to the phone, was the business card that the *Holden Herald* reporter had left behind. He picked it up and turned it over in his hand.

'You didn't call this guy, did you?' he asked, more to change the subject than anything else.

It worked better than he had expected. Asha looked unusually shifty. 'Well . . .' she began.

'Well, what?'

'Well . . . I didn't want to tell you until it was all arranged. But we got talking the other day.' Asha paused and bit her lip. The words came tumbling out all at once, so quickly that it took Sal a second to understand them. 'And he offered me an internship at the *Herald*.'

'Are you kidding me?' Sal asked, horror-struck. 'You can't work for them.'

'It's a great opportunity, Sal,' Asha protested. 'This could be really good for me. You know I've always wanted to be a journalist. And now I'm not going to uni, I need to start getting some experience.'

Sal gaped at her. 'But you already *have* a job. What about the shop?'

Asha narrowed her eyes. 'Please don't be difficult about this, Salem. I'm doing it.'

Lost for words, Sal opened his mouth, closed it again, turned on his heel and climbed the stairs. He slammed his bedroom door behind him and threw himself on to the nest of blankets that Pax had left in the middle of the floor.

In the dead of night, a haunted house is the very last place you should be.

The house is old, and sometimes it's hard to tell if the groans you are hearing are the groans of a ghost, or just the groans of ancient plumbing gurgling into life. If the flickering lights are the work of a phantom, or the failings of a faulty fuse box.

As you lie in bed, the dark is threaded with the anticipation of what is to come.

You know your sleep will be interrupted by the sounds of things long lost but not quite gone. On a good night, you can clench your eyes closed, twist the sheets in your hands and wait, heart racing, for the moment to end. On a good night, you fall into fitful sleep, and don't wake until dawn.

But not every night is a good night.

CHAPTER FIFTEEN

Dirk was in an exuberant mood on Monday morning. He insisted on eating in the cafeteria at lunchtime, convinced that his Halloween party masterplan would have sparked some kind of social revolution. They sat down at an empty table and Dirk waved at a group of his football mates who nodded and waved back at him. One even ran over to high-five him. Then they walked away and sat at the opposite end of the room.

'Why do I feel like people still don't like us?' Dirk asked, visibly deflating. He pushed his plate of pizza away. There were six slices today, stacked into a greasy, unappetizing tower.

'They like you fine,' Sal said.

'Yeah,' Dirk agreed impatiently. 'What I'm trying to say – no offence – is why does nobody like *you three*?'

'It's probably my fault,' Pax piped up, looking sheepish. He was wearing a pair of mustard-coloured cords and a jumper emblazoned with a knitted rabbit. He had brought a jar of pickles with him and he was busy piling them into his peanut butter sandwich. 'Some people think I'm strange.'

'At least they don't think you're a slut,' Elsie said, stabbing her fork into her pile of chips. She dunked one in a pool of ketchup and bit it viciously in two.

'Or possessed by a ghost,' Sal said.

'Which is totally ridiculous.' Pax was clearly gearing up for one of his rambling lectures on All Things Spooky. 'They're confusing them with demons. Ghost possessions are *incredibly* rare.'

'I really thought the party would work,' Dirk said.

He was still looking very sulky, but Elsie pushed his pizza stack back towards him and he started chewing mournfully.

Elsie shrugged. 'At least we had a good time.'

'Some more than others,' Sal said, remembering Dirk disappearing upstairs with Jo. 'I'd tell Asha if I thought she'd give a damn.'

Dirk nearly choked on his pizza, throat convulsing in his efforts to speak. 'You can't,' he eventually spluttered. 'I love her.'

Everyone turned to stare at him, and his skin turned beetroot red. Elsie was staring at him in incredulous disbelief. Pax's brow had furrowed in sympathy.

'I mean, I like her a lot, y'know,' Dirk corrected. 'And Jo's got a crush on *you*, Sal. Which you were being a dick about, by the way. So really we were just drowning our sorrows in each other . . . which is kind of poetic when you think about it.'

He looked around the table for reassurance but none was forthcoming. Instead, Elsie and Pax seemed to be having an elaborate conversation with the use of only their eyebrows. Elsie looked as if she was trying hard not to laugh.

Sal wrinkled his nose. 'You getting laid is *never* going to be poetic.'

'It will be with Asha,' Dirk said.

Sal leant over the table and hit him around the head with his history textbook.

The four of them went back to Dirk's house after school to help him tidy before his parents got home. The house was strewn with plastic cups and empty bottles, and fake cobwebs were still hanging sadly from the ceiling. People had been smoking in the kitchen and the sink was littered with cigarette butts.

'You could have started this yesterday,' Sal grumbled, as he brushed crisps out from between the sofa cushions.

'I did,' Dirk said, shuddering. He had put on a pair of pink rubber gloves and was reluctantly collecting beer bottles. 'And I was right, by the way. Someone threw up in one of the pumpkins.'

Elsie turned pink. 'God,' she said weakly. 'Who would *do* that?'

'Oh, don't worry about it,' Pax said. 'Sal nearly threw up on *me*.'

Sal had been hoping that Pax had forgotten about that. He glowered over at him, and Pax pouted back, eyes twinkling. Dirk chuckled to himself, looking instantly more cheerful.

'I thought you had your dance thing after school today?' Sal asked Elsie, keen to change the subject.

Excitement over the winter dance had reached a feverish pitch. People were pairing up left, right and centre. In a burst of paranoia Sal had spent the past couple of weeks ducking his head and disappearing whenever girls looked like they might be about to approach him in the corridors.

Elsie looked up at him and pushed her hair out of her eyes in order to better fix him with a scowl.

'Mrs Macmillan heard about me slapping Jacob in the cafeteria.'

Sal winced, remembering Dirk telling him about Jacob and Elsie's very dramatic, very *public* break-up. 'And?'

'And she said I'd acted in a way that didn't represent the values of the school. So she kicked me off the winter dance committee.'

'Lucky you,' Sal said, before he could stop himself.

'Yes, well,' Elsie said with a sniff. 'It *was* kind of stupid. I was only really going because Jacob wanted to.'

'Right.'

'*And*,' she continued, gathering steam. Her cheeks were flushed and she looked around at them defiantly, pushing a frizzy lock of hair out of her face. 'I'd just found a local artist who might have been willing to create an ice sculpture within our budget. So, *really*, the joke's on them.'

'It is,' Dirk said, catching Sal's eye and winking.

Sal grinned. 'It really is.'

Pax was looking between them with wide eyes, twisting his hands together. 'There's . . . going to be a winter dance?' he asked.

Dirk frowned at him. 'December the twelfth. How did you not know that?'

'No one talks to me,' Pax reminded him in a matter-of-fact voice.

'Oh, right.' Dirk nodded at him, as if this was something he was well aware of but had momentarily forgotten and not found at all strange until now. 'Well, it's just a bit of a joke really. Everyone sneaks in booze and people always end up hooking up in empty classrooms.'

Pax's eyes got even wider. '*Wow*,' he said. 'Do I need someone to go with?'

'Well, *yeah*,' Dirk said.

Elsie frowned at him. 'No, you don't.' She linked her arm through Pax's. 'We can go on our own together.'

'You could ask Niall,' Dirk said cheerfully, ignoring Elsie's suggestion. '*He's* gay.'

Niall was a year eleven boy, and the only non-closeted gay kid in the school. He also had an unhealthy obsession with *Game of Thrones* and looked, Sal had always thought, a bit like a weasel. Pax looked more than a little taken aback at having been outed to the room and simultaneously paired up with someone he had never even met. He glanced at Sal, who turned the full force of his scowl on Dirk.

'*Or* you can ask people from outside school,' Dirk said hastily. He met Sal's eye, looking unusually nervous. 'Do you reckon Asha would go with me?'

'I think she'd rather dance with an armadillo.'

'Yeah,' Dirk said. He stared sadly down at the half-empty beer bottles he had been clearing off the coffee table and absent-mindedly took a swig. 'That's what I thought.'

CHAPTER SIXTEEN

Early in November, Sal arrived at school one morning to discover the reporter from the *Holden Herald*, Faris Jones, had run a new article on his house. He wrote about its previous owners, listing their names and how they had died, speculating on who might now be responsible for the hauntings. He'd stopped short of naming Sal's own family, and there was no mention of his father, or how he had died. But Sal's relief at this concession was overshadowed by his annoyance. There were photographs too . . . of the gargoyles that framed the porch, the nearby yew trees stretching their arms towards freedom and the twisting ivy that crawled over the front gate.

Sal read the article through once, and then tossed the paper in the nearest bin and spat his chewing gum out on top of it. Asha had begun her internship at the *Herald* that same day and, though he knew it was unreasonable, he couldn't quite overcome the sense of betrayal.

The pointing and muttering in the corridors got worse, and people started moving out of his way when they saw him coming, as if he might be contagious. The sixth-form students were the worst of all. They thought the entire situation was laughable and, for some unfathomable reason, that he might actually be enjoying the attention. In response they either ignored him or treated him with sneering disdain.

He grew surlier in response, keeping his jaw clenched and his eyes on the floor. He scowled at anyone who looked like they might be threatening to speak to him. Even Pax who, along with Elsie and Dirk, was one of the only people who still tried to engage him in conversation.

'Are you often in the newspaper?' Pax asked him that lunchtime in the library. Dirk and Elsie were busy arguing in the corner and they had moved away to get some peace under the pretence of browsing the books.

Sal glared at him. 'I'm *not* in the newspaper.'

'Your house, I mean,' Pax clarified.

'It comes up every so often.'

'When did it start?'

Sal was rapidly losing interest in the conversation. 'I can't remember.'

Pax looked astonished. 'But don't you keep the articles?'

'Yeah,' Sal said, dryly. 'We frame them.'

'Ooh.' Pax's eyes had lit up with excitement. 'Can I see the others?'

125

'*No*. I was kidding.'

'Oh, right.' Pax paused, then tilted his head and fixed Sal with a contemplative look. 'Am I annoying you?'

Sal gave that some consideration. Pax had been rambling on at him for nearly twenty minutes, filling him in on everything from Aloysius's new feeding schedule to the most effective spells to cast under a crescent moon.

'No,' he said, surprised to find he was telling the truth. 'No, you're not.'

'Oh, good.' Pax's expression cleared. 'Because my mum says to invite you to dinner.'

'Oh.' Sal frowned, flicking through the book in his hands. It looked like one that Pax might like and he handed it over to him. 'I don't know. I'm busy.'

'When?' Pax asked, accepting the book without looking at it.

'When are you asking me?'

'When you're not busy.'

Sal made his signature grumbling noise under his breath, which Pax had long since worked out was all bark and no bite.

'She thinks you're avoiding her,' he said. 'Don't tell her I told you that.'

Sal *was*, in fact, avoiding her. He hadn't forgotten the way she had shouted down the phone when Pax had slept over after the Halloween party. He wasn't entirely certain he'd still be welcome at Pax's house and he hadn't been over since. Their long afternoons spent lazing around in Pax's bedroom had become a thing of the past.

'I told her nothing happened,' Pax said. 'At Halloween. If that's what you're worried about.'

Sal glowered at him. 'Why would anything have happened?'

Pax's already flushed cheeks instantly turned a deep tomato-red. 'It wouldn't,' he said hurriedly. 'It won't. Probably.'

Feeling guilty for having embarrassed Pax, Sal decided to ignore the *probably*.

'Will there be pudding?' Sal asked, remembering the smell of baking that so often filled Pax's house. His mouth started watering.

'Of course there will,' Pax said, looking appalled at the question. 'Tonight?'

Sal hesitated, then nodded. 'Tonight.'

When Sal got home that evening, Asha had a copy of the *Holden Herald*. She was hunched over the kitchen table reading the article about their house so intently that her nose nearly touched the paper. Sal half expected her to start taking notes. She had just returned from the first day of her internship, and she was wearing a suit jacket instead of her usual shop apron. The sight of it irritated him almost as much as the article.

'Why are you reading that?' he asked. 'You live here.'

Asha pushed the newspaper away. 'Seems like a pretty good reason to read it. I want to know what he's saying about us.'

'I thought you'd already know,' Sal said, unable to keep

the accusatory tone out of his voice. 'Don't you work there now?'

'No,' Asha said. She pursed her lips. 'It's an internship. I mostly just make the coffee. And I've only been there a day.'

Sal dropped his backpack on the floor. He was busy stuffing dry cereal into his mouth when he realized Asha was still watching him. He raised a questioning eyebrow. If she was waiting for him to ask how her day had gone, she was just going to have to keep waiting. He wasn't interested.

'Do you ever wonder . . .' she began, then trailed off.

'What?'

'Well, I've been thinking . . .' She glanced back down at the newspaper article. 'It's *our* life. Wouldn't it be better if we told our own story?'

'I can think of, literally, nothing worse,' Sal said. As far as he was concerned, the ghosts, the hauntings and the noises at night weren't anyone else's business. Every house had its secrets. Some were just louder than others. He pulled a box of cigarettes from his back pocket and lit one solely for the purpose of irritating Asha.

She pulled it out of his hands and stubbed it out in the sink. 'We can't go on like this for ever, Sal.'

Sal glared back at her. 'Like what?'

'Ever since Dad died,' Asha said, 'we've just been ignoring all the bad stuff. Pretending it isn't happening.'

'Everyone does that,' Sal said. 'That's just how you do life.'

Asha shook her head. She was still clutching the newspaper in one hand. 'Well maybe it shouldn't be.'

Sal pulled the newspaper out of her hand, screwed it up and threw it in the sink alongside the crumpled cigarette. He turned on the tap and they stood and watched it dissolve into a pulp.

'You think too much,' he told her.

Asha lifted a soggy strand of paper from the sink and sighed. '*You* don't think at all.'

CHAPTER SEVENTEEN

When Sal told Asha he was going out to dinner, she looked momentarily astounded.

'Like a sociable person?' she asked.

'You can talk,' Sal grumbled.

'OK,' she said slowly. She opened the fridge and poked suspiciously at the contents. It was empty, save for a jar of pickles and a few sad-looking vegetables, which were slowly rotting away on the bottom shelf. 'See if you can bring home leftovers.'

Pax's mother opened the door when he rang the bell an hour later. She was wearing a long floral dress in rich autumn colours and a big burgundy cardigan. Sal felt scruffy in his usual jeans and hoodie combo. He had stood on the doorstep for a full minute before ringing the doorbell, bouncing up and down to ease his nerves, and was now slightly sweaty and unkempt. He tried to edge around her, but she reached out and ruffled his hair, more firmly than was really necessary.

'I'm glad you're here,' she said sternly. 'Pax has always had trouble making friends.'

'Are you sure?' Sal asked. 'He didn't give *me* much of a choice.'

Pax's mother continued to stare at him and Sal averted his gaze, feeling distinctly awkward.

'He's very fond of you, Salem.' She pronounced his name correctly.

She ushered him through the door and into the kitchen before he could embarrass himself with a response. Pax was sitting cross-legged on the work surface and appeared to have also dressed up for the occasion. He was swamped in a very fluffy white jumper and his hair was sticking out in all directions in a mass of frizzy, untamed curls.

'You look like a cloud,' Sal said before he could bite his tongue.

Pax's mother made a soft noise of approval behind him, as if he had said something very sweet.

'Wow, thanks,' Pax said. 'You look like . . .' He tilted his head to one side and looked Sal up and down. 'You.'

Pax's mother gestured at Sal to take a seat at the tiny kitchen table and bustled over to the stove, where she appeared to have at least five different pans on the go. The kitchen was warm with steam, and the windows had clouded with condensation. It smelt delicious. She pushed Pax off the countertop with the end of a wooden spoon and set him to work helping her serve the food.

Sal folded his arms over his chest and tried hard not to appear uncomfortable. Within five minutes, it had stopped being an effort. Pax's mother insisted on him calling her Annie. She was even more talkative than Pax, and the two of them carried an entire conversation that somehow managed to include him but also meant he barely had to say anything. Sal wasn't required to do anything much apart from nod his head and smile at the appropriate moments. When Annie asked him questions, Pax jumped in and answered them for him, his answers unnervingly accurate.

She had made a root vegetable stew and dumplings, and it was one of the most comforting meals Sal had ever eaten. He asked Pax how he managed to stay so skinny, and Annie beamed at him before producing an apple crumble from the oven.

'He gets it from his father,' Annie told him. Her smile faded a touch as she spoke. 'He looks just like him too. He's very busy with work these days, so we don't see much of him.'

'He's a postman,' Pax told Sal, as if he thought this was a very unusual and exotic thing to be.

'Hm,' Sal said. He had no interest in talking about Pax's father. He thought the man was an idiot for abandoning his family, for abandoning Pax. He smiled politely and tucked into the gargantuan portion of crumble and custard that Annie put on the table in front of him.

They went upstairs after dinner and, in the interest of not making things awkward, both pretended they hadn't noticed Annie mouthing *Leave the door open* at Pax. They took steaming cups of tea with them and sat on the cramped little window seat under the skylight.

There was a book on palmistry on the floor nearby, and Sal reached over to pick it up, thumbing through it with interest.

'You know this is bullshit, right?' he asked, pausing to inspect an intricately sketched diagram.

Pax quirked an eyebrow at him. 'Why are you reading it, then?'

Sal set the book to one side and outstretched his right hand, palm up, in silent challenge.

Pax looked taken aback. 'I could tell you anything and you won't know if I'm right or not,' he said, taking hold of his hand. 'Not for years anyway.'

'I'll write to you before I die and let you know.'

'Oh, OK,' Pax said, expression clearing. 'That's a good idea.'

He traced a finger along Sal's palm, sending a pleasant tingling sensation skittering across his skin, and peered at the lines as if reading a map. It was quiet in the room, and Sal closed his eyes and listened to the sound of Pax's breathing, and the clatter of pots and pans being washed in the kitchen below.

'What's your diagnosis?' Sal asked, after a full minute of silence had passed.

'Instability and inner turmoil.' Pax looked up and caught Sal's eye. 'And a tendency to be really quite grumpy.'

Sal's laugh escaped him before he could prevent it. He sank back against the wall behind him and looked sleepily around the room. Pax's fingers continued to trail over his skin, drawing swirling patterns without any apparent rhyme or reason. A selection of photos were pinned to the wall behind his head. A pale-skinned man with Pax's blond hair stared back at him. He had nearly the same eyes, but they didn't suit him like they suited Pax. They were too wide for his face and made him look lost.

'So . . .' Sal cleared his throat. 'Are you gonna tell me why you moved here, now?'

'We used to live in London,' Pax said. 'But we couldn't afford the house after Dad left.'

Sal didn't know what to say to that. He settled for keeping quiet and, as usual, Pax hurried to fill the silence.

'Mum's always wanted to live in the country. And we thought it would be nice to have a fresh start.' He hesitated, looking mildly embarrassed. 'I didn't really fit in at my old school.'

Sal swallowed down the urge to tell Pax he didn't fit in at his new school either. 'Your dad's an idiot,' he said instead.

Pax let go of his hand and frowned at him. 'What?'

'I just don't know why anyone wouldn't want to be around you.' Silently he thought it was better to have a father who had died than one who had decided to live without him.

Pax's mouth curved up into a rueful half-smile. '*You* didn't want to be around me at first,' he pointed out.

'Yeah, well,' Sal said, feeling guilty because that was true. And guiltier still because he had thought Pax hadn't noticed. 'I'm an idiot too.'

When he looked back at him, Pax was biting his lip and his eyes were shining too brightly. Sal leant forward and biffed him gently on the nose to cheer him up.

It wasn't until he got home that night that Sal realized Annie hadn't asked about the ghosts. He didn't know if Pax had told her about the article. But Annie hadn't mentioned the house once, or wanted to know if it was really haunted. Instead she wanted to know the answers to inane questions like his favourite subject at school, and whether he played sports, and if he liked Pax's new hat, and did he want any more apple crumble?

He got the impression she still thought he was Pax's boyfriend. But he was too warm and sleepy and full to care.

CHAPTER EIGHTEEN

Friday the 6th of November was the night of the village bonfire. It was cold and damp. The air felt heavy and the entire village lay shrouded in mist. Sal sat and stared out of his bedroom window, eyes glued to the gate at the bottom of the drive. It was getting dark and he could only just see through the gloom. Asha was working late at the shop and in the attic above him he could hear the radio blaring in his mum's studio. She always left it on while she worked, even at night. She said it helped her concentrate, but Sal thought it was to cover the noise of the house. The sound of ghostly muttering voices.

At the bottom of the drive, Pax appeared through the mist and Sal scrambled into his jacket and took the stairs three at a time. He flung the door open just as Pax had lifted his hand to bang on it. He knocked on Sal's chest instead, grinning.

'Hey,' Sal said, stepping outside and pulling the door closed behind him. He gave Pax a gentle push down the porch steps. 'Let's go.'

The smell of damp wood and acrid smoke was thick in the air and the distant pop of fireworks had begun. A multicoloured scattering of sparks flickered above the town in the distance. Sal slung an arm around Pax's shoulders as they walked, breathing in the damp autumn air and tilting his head back to feel the lightly falling drizzle on his face. He dug his fingers into the fur of Pax's coat and scratched lightly against the grain.

Pax made a purring sound and grinned at him. He was wearing his reindeer hat again, casting his face into shadow, but his eyes glinted through the gloom.

They stopped at the shop because Pax wanted marshmallows. He was a vegetarian but he informed Sal that he made an exception for confectionery.

'I'm pretty sure that's cheating,' Sal said, as they stepped through the door.

The shop's fluorescent lights were almost blindingly bright after their walk through the dark. Asha was behind the counter, chewing gum and flicking through a new edition of the *Herald*. She looked tired, Sal thought. She had spent the week travelling into town to work at the *Herald* during the day, and then coming home to work at the shop in the evenings. There were dark circles beneath her eyes, and she didn't bother making a snarky comment at the sight of him. Instead, she snapped her gum and blew a bright pink bubble the size of her own face.

'Wow,' Pax said, mouth dropping open. 'You *have* to show me how to do that.'

Sal grabbed hold of him before Asha could hand him a stick of the bubble gum, dragging him down the aisles. He pulled him into the confectionery aisle for a giant bag of marshmallows and to the fridge for two bottles of cider.

'ID?' Asha said in a bored voice when Sal set the alcohol down on the counter.

'Oh, come *on*,' Sal groaned.

She smirked and scanned the bottles through the till.

'Are you coming to the bonfire later?' Pax asked her.

He was bopping up and down on his tiptoes in excitement. Sal placed a hand on his shoulder to keep him in one place.

'If I wanted to watch teenagers getting drunk and making out in the dark,' Asha said, 'I would have gone to university.'

Sal rolled his eyes and tucked the bottles of cider under his coat. Asha would have given her left foot to go to university, and they both knew it. 'Bye, Asha.'

She shot them a brief, tight smile. 'Have fun.'

'I'll tell Dirk you said hi,' Pax told her, as Sal dragged him away.

She lifted her newspaper again and regarded them steadily from behind it. 'Please don't.'

They followed the orange glow of the fire across the village square, past the churchyard and across the stile into the field beyond. The bonfire was bigger than Pax's house and they could feel the heat as soon as they entered the field, boots slipping on the muddy grass.

'Why *didn't* Asha go to university?' Pax asked, as they picked their way across the grass. He opened the bag of marshmallows, rustling it loudly, and stuffed one into his mouth. 'Did she not get in?'

'She got in,' Sal said. It came out sounding snappier than he had intended. 'But we had family stuff. She couldn't go.'

'Oh,' Pax mumbled around his marshmallow. 'What sort of family stuff?'

'My mum's not been doing so well,' Sal said. 'Since my dad died. Asha kind of needs to be around right now.'

Pax frowned. 'I thought your dad died five years ago?'

'So what, she should just get over it?'

'Sorry,' said Pax quickly. 'Of course not.' After a pause, he said, 'She should start in January instead. Asha, I mean. My cousin did that.'

'Huh,' Sal said, frowning down at the ground through the darkness. 'I didn't know you could do that.'

'I think sometimes they make exceptions. Does Asha know? You should tell her.'

'No point,' Sal said, truthfully enough. 'She won't listen.'

It had given him another idea, though. He filed it away in the back of his mind, ready for later examination.

They wound their way through the crowds, avoiding the squealing children racing between the legs of their parents. There was a group of Holden High students on the opposite side of the fire, standing too close and already tossing empty bottles into the flames. The smell of weed floated towards them through the dark. They found Dirk and Elsie lurking on the edge of the group and, as usual, they were arguing.

They ate hot buttered potatoes out of tin foil, for a pound each from a makeshift kiosk on the edge of the field. Their skins were black, the butter hot enough to burn Sal's fingers, and each mouthful was laced with salt.

Then they toasted marshmallows on the smouldering edges of the fire, staking them on bark-stripped twigs and holding them to the flame until the outsides had blistered and the insides had turned to sweet, sticky goo.

Sal could fit seven giant marshmallows in his mouth at once. Pax could only manage five, and Elsie beat all of them with eight. Dirk said this made sense because she was the loudest and she punched him on the arm in response. Two minutes later, he was chasing her at a sprint across the field, leaving Sal and Pax alone on the outskirts of the bonfire's glow.

Sal barely noticed the two of them leaving. He found Pax's presence did something strange where it seemed to make everyone around him fade into non-existence. Including, sometimes, himself. It was kind of freeing, and he didn't mind it at all. It made him feel like he was floating. They were sharing a bottle of cider which, though cold from the fridge, was rapidly turning warm from the heat of the fire and the blanket of their hands wrapped around it.

Sal was wearing a tatty old pair of black fingerless gloves that he'd bought years ago in a short-lived but very embarrassing goth phase, and Pax was obviously getting a kick out of making fun of them.

'Aren't your fingers cold?' he asked, taking Sal's hand in his own to examine it with concern.

'Nope.' Sal shook him off, laughing at his expression. 'Aren't *you* too warm?' he retaliated.

It was hot on the edges of the fire. Sal's nose was beginning to feel like it might be blistering from the heat.

Pax was dressed in his furry coat, a thick woollen hat and mittens that made his hands look twice their actual size. He looked down at them and grimaced in defeat before peeling them off and stuffing them into his pockets.

'Maybe just a little.'

They moved away from the fire towards a copse of trees at the edge of the field, where the air was cooler. It was quieter too, but the sound of crackling wood and laughter floated towards them on the breeze. They could just make out the flickering faces of the crowd, half in shadow.

Fireworks screeched overhead and they looked up to see red and gold sparks exploding above them. It was followed by a cacophony of light and noise, and several panicked screams, when one firework tipped over and skimmed the heads of the crowd in a fiery blaze.

Pax was watching with his hands clasped tightly over his ears, and Sal was doing his best not to find it endearing. He was saying something, half shouting over the screeching of rockets, but his voice was whipped away by the wind and Sal found himself staring at his mouth in an effort to understand him. He looked away, tilting his head up to watch as the last of the red and gold sparks disintegrated into nothingness in the velvety black sky.

When he looked back, Pax was suddenly, bizarrely, close. Close enough for Sal to count the powdery smattering of freckles across his nose and see the flecks of hazel in his grey eyes. There was only a centimetre of space between them. He leant in.

The first thing he noticed was that Pax's lips were chapped. The second was that they tasted of marshmallows.

Kissing Pax was a sensation unlike anything Sal had ever felt before. But it wasn't until they had lost their footing and stumbled back against the trunk of the nearest tree that he realized he didn't find it strange at all.

Pax's hands were on his neck, along his jaw, in his hair. His nose was very cold and his mouth was very warm. Somewhere in the background, Dirk and Elsie were laughing, but Sal didn't care enough to stop. He took a step back and pulled Pax further into the shadows.

The next time they looked up the fire had died down to embers and the field was nearly deserted. The fog had cleared and the night was near freezing but Sal was still warm from the afterglow of the fire, the cider and Pax's stupidly oversized but incredibly soft fur coat.

'Wow,' Pax said.

Sal frowned and tucked an escaped curl of hair back under the boy's hat. He thought *wow* just about covered it. 'Yeah.'

★

They walked home together, and it occurred to Sal, halfway there, that he might finally have found a way to shut Pax up. The boy hadn't said more than two words to him since they'd kissed. He was still looking dazed when they arrived at Pax's front door.

'Well,' Sal said, beginning to wonder if Pax was regretting what had happened. He looked down and kicked the dying leaves off the doorstep. 'Goodnight, then.'

He turned to leave and Pax's hands landed on either side of his face, turning him back around. He kissed him again, and they ended up sprawled against the front door. Sal pushed his hands under Pax's hat to get to his hair and Pax giggled against his mouth.

They were interrupted by a light flicking on in an upstairs window, and Sal leapt guiltily backwards, making Pax laugh harder.

'Shut up,' Sal said, grinning reluctantly.

Pax opened the door and slipped inside. 'Goodnight, Salem.'

Sal watched the door close behind him, stuck to the spot and contending with the uncomfortable sensation that his insides might be melting. 'Goodnight.'

Not every night is a good night. Some nights, you lie awake in the darkness.

It is raining hard and freezing cold, the wind whipping at your bed sheets. The window you had closed before bed has been flung open. Through it, not a light can be seen for miles. The rest of the village is sleeping.

Suddenly, there is someone in your room, standing at the foot of your bed. Someone you recognize, and who you know is long gone. Everything about them is familiar, from the shadows of their face to their voice when they say goodnight.

They reach out to tuck you in.

You wrestle one hand free from the covers, reaching for the lamp on the bedside table. Your fingers falter over cool metal as you fumble for the switch.

When the lights turn on, the ghost disappears.

CHAPTER NINETEEN

Sal awoke the next morning to the sound of his phone chiming.

Pax had sent him three texts in quick succession. One to say good morning. One with a gif of an uncurling hedgehog. And a third to ask if he could see Sal later.

Sal's stomach flipped over as he stared down at his phone, his mind immediately whisking him back to Pax's doorstep, reliving the press of his lips. He frowned at the texts. Then he groaned and shoved the phone back under his pillow.

In the harsh light of day, kissing Pax suddenly didn't seem like such a good idea. Sal's life was complicated enough already. He wasn't sure he was ready to drag anyone else into it. Especially not someone as weird as Pax, who knitted his own clothes and confused everyone he met.

There was one small problem. Kissing Pax had felt good.

Really good, in fact. A dizzy, drunken kind of good that Sal would really have liked to blame on the cider they'd been drinking. But he didn't have a hangover. His head wasn't throbbing. In fact, they hadn't even finished the bottle. Pax had dropped it when Sal kissed him. It was probably still lying in the grass under the trees, forgotten.

He sank back into the pillows and tried not to picture the way Pax's face looked, with his lips parted and his eyes closed. It swam tauntingly in front of his vision until he growled in annoyance and pressed his fists against his eyelids, so hard that white spots blurred the darkness beneath them.

His phone chimed again. It was a novel-length text from Elsie, which he didn't bother reading. It consisted mostly of emojis and exclamation marks, and he already had enough of those swirling around his head without anyone else's input. He got out of bed and went downstairs to make a cup of coffee, leaving his phone behind.

The house was gloomy and dark, and the kitchen was empty. There was a soft scuffling noise as he walked in; the resident mouse scampering away, somewhere behind the kitchen cupboards. Asha had already left for work in the shop. She'd been out on one of her early morning coffee runs and picked up a doughnut for him from the bakery in the village. She'd left it on the table with a Post-it note on top, on which she'd scribbled: *See you later, loser – A*. Next to it was Asha's takeaway cup, drained to the dregs, and a battered old paperback. The title *How to Get Published: Writing What You Know* was emblazoned in bright yellow letters across the front.

Forgetting for a moment about Pax, Sal was hit by a sudden surge of guilt. He thought of the dark shadows that seemed to have become permanently etched under Asha's eyes. He thought too of the fact she was working two jobs, and earning less money, but still spending it on things to make him smile. He felt bad for having told her to pass up the internship – the single opportunity she'd taken to do something for herself. The sight of the dough-nut was making him feel worse. He swallowed it in three bites, and it dragged in his throat on the way down.

Brushing powdered sugar off the front of his hoodie, he was reminded of an idea he'd had the night before. He raced back upstairs, taking the stairs two at a time, hesi-tated on the landing, and slipped through the half-open door to Asha's room. Her desk was a mess of crumpled paper: typed pages that she had printed out and scrawled over so much that they had become unintelligible. He rummaged through her desk drawer and lifted out the university prospectus with the neatly folded acceptance letter still clasped within its pages. He stuffed it under his jumper, took the stairs in three giant leaps and pulled on his jacket in the hallway.

It had rained overnight and grey clouds hung low on the horizon. The ivy glistened and dewdrops clung to the cobwebs that framed the porch. Sal flicked them free as he passed, sending them cascading to the ground, where they shattered like beads of glass. He paused when he reached the broken gate at the end of the drive, looking left and right before climbing over. He didn't think he could handle running into Pax just yet. He wasn't avoiding him, he told himself, just creating some distance. He couldn't think straight when they were together. Or within a few hundred metres of each other.

Mrs Helliwell glared at him from behind her net curtains as he walked down the lane. At the coffee shop in the village square he stopped and bought himself a triple-shot Americano. The further he got from home, the better he felt. When he reached Dirk's house, he banged on the door.

Dirk's mother opened it and smiled at the sight of him before shouting Dirk's name. He emerged from the kitchen holding a sharing bag of Doritos and steadily munching his way through them. He grinned when he saw Sal on the doorstep, revealing a mouthful of bright orange mush.

'Hey, Romeo.'

'I need your help,' Sal said, entering before he was invited. 'Don't tell anyone I said that, ever.'

'OK,' Dirk said. 'What with?'

'I need to borrow your laptop. I'm writing to King's College London.'

Dirk frowned at him, putting the handful of Doritos he was holding back in the bag. He wiped his mouth with his sleeve, looking concerned. 'I thought you didn't want to go to uni?'

'It's not for me,' Sal said, pulling off his trainers and setting off up the stairs.

Dirk's room was even messier than his own – the bed was unmade and the carpet strewn with unwashed football kits. The walls were covered in posters of bands and famous athletes. There was an extensive comic book collection in a bookcase in the corner, which Dirk never mentioned and (Sal had learnt the hard way) did not appreciate being teased for. Grey the Labrador was snoring softly in the corner.

'So who's it for?' Dirk asked, standing in the doorway and watching with a frown as Sal sat down on the bed and opened his laptop. 'Don't check my internet history.'

'I'd rather die. And it's for Asha.'

'Aw, neat.' Dirk's eyes lit up. He threw himself on to the bed and tried to wrestle the laptop out of Sal's hands. 'Can I write it?'

'No,' Sal said. 'Absolutely not.'

He pulled the prospectus out from under his jumper and laid it carefully on Dirk's checked bed sheets, pulling out the letter. He reread it in full before taking a deep breath and copying the return address on to the top of a Word document.

'You stick your tongue out when you're typing,' Dirk said. 'And what's with all the secret squirrel stuff, anyway?'

'She doesn't know I'm sending it,' Sal said, shrugging.

Dirk picked up the acceptance letter and read it with a furrowed brow.

'Says here she's already got in,' he said, once he'd reached the end of the first line, as if Sal might not have noticed.

'Yes.' Sal grabbed the letter back and attempted to rub off the dusty Dorito-orange fingerprints that Dirk had left on the edges. 'But that was for September. She's missed the intake. I'm writing to see if she can start in January.'

Dirk was frowning. 'Why?'

'Because she wants to go,' Sal said. 'And I know she won't do it herself.'

He took a large gulp of his takeaway coffee and tapped away at the keys. Dirk, for once, stayed quiet while he wrote, save for the incessant crunching of crisps. Twenty minutes later Sal typed *Yours Faithfully, Asha Rose Amani*, then he hit the print button, and forged Asha's signature on the end of the letter.

'I'm pretty sure that's illegal,' Dirk said, shaking the last of the Dorito crumbs out of the bag and straight into his mouth.

'I'm pretty sure it isn't,' Sal said, though the possibility hadn't actually occurred to him. He looked down at the letter and shrugged. 'You got an envelope?'

'So,' Dirk said, when Sal was busy licking the envelope. He waggled his eyebrows suggestively. 'You and Pax, huh?'

Sal could tell that Dirk had been dying to mention this since he had arrived. He frowned back at him. 'What about me and Pax?'

He was used to talking to Dirk about *girls*. Dirk had

spent the past year hassling him about Jo. Although those conversations usually ended with Sal changing the subject and Dirk looking at him like he'd grown an extra head. Sal hadn't expected him to think that Pax merited the same level of enthusiasm. He wasn't sure whether he was relieved or not.

'Did you do it?' Dirk asked brazenly.

'*No*,' Sal protested, feeling his cheeks burning at the thought. He was pretty sure the tips of his ears had turned red, and he scrubbed his hands over them self-consciously. '*God*. We just kissed . . . a lot.'

He hadn't ever *done it*. Hadn't even got close. He'd got his hand half under a girl's skirt once and panicked and had to take it back out again. Unfortunately, his lack of experience with sex didn't stop Dirk wanting to talk about it.

'So are you guys, like, *together* now?' Dirk asked.

Sal's stomach lurched. He pressed down again on the seal of the envelope, although it was already neatly closed. 'Dunno.'

Dirk chuckled and fell back to sprawl on the bed. He stretched his long limbs out lazily. 'Dude,' he said. 'You *are*. That is so weird.'

Sal scowled. 'What is?'

'Just . . .' Dirk hesitated, looking like someone who had skated on to very thin ice without realizing and was debating the safest way to get back to shore. 'You and Pax being, y'know, you *and* Pax. Sal and Pax.'

When Dirk put it like that, it didn't sound like much at

all. It definitely didn't sound bad. In fact, it sounded pretty good.

'Yeah.' Sal ducked his head to hide his grin as he stuck a first-class stamp to the front of the envelope. 'Me and Pax.'

When he left Dirk's house, the clouds on the horizon had receded and he found himself blinking into bright wintery sunlight. He fished his phone out of his pocket and stared down at Pax's texts again as he walked.

Halfway down the street he tripped over a loose stone. He sank down on to a low wall nearby and finally typed out a reply.

CHAPTER TWENTY

It should have been awkward, Sal thought, when Pax turned up on his doorstep that evening. He was wearing the same hat he had worn when they first met – the one with the plaited tassels – and Sal remembered disliking him and wondered how everything had changed so quickly.

But Pax didn't give him a chance to feel weird about it.

'Should I come in?' he asked, already edging through the door. 'Or are you coming to mine?'

'Presumptuous,' Sal said as he stamped his way into his trainers. He glanced behind him to check Asha wasn't lurking anywhere within earshot.

'Not really,' Pax said. He tipped his head to one side and smiled, looking very smug. 'You kissed me first.'

Sal pressed a hand to Pax's mouth and pushed him out

of the door, closing it hurriedly behind them. They stood sheltered in the porch, between the grimacing gargoyles. The driveway and the lane beyond were deserted.

'You were all up in my face,' Sal said, feeling strangely defensive. 'What was I supposed to do?'

Pax leant in and pressed his face, nose to nose, against Sal's. He was so close that Sal could smell the minty waft of his toothpaste. 'Hi,' he said.

Sal grinned and looked away, suddenly nervous. 'Hi.'

'I came round earlier,' Pax said. 'But you weren't here.'

'I was at Dirk's,' Sal said.

'Oh.' Pax's smile wavered. 'OK.'

They walked down the lane together to Pax's house, kicking through the crunchy autumn leaves. Pax was wearing a scarf so long it trailed among them, creating a rustling sound as they walked. When they entered the cottage, Annie looked up from her spot at the kitchen table. She was filling in the crossword and shot them a look that made it clear that Pax had told her everything. There was a knowing smile tugging at the corners of her lips.

'Hello, Salem,' she said.

'Hi,' Sal said, turning to glare suspiciously at Pax.

Pax shrugged, his cheeks pink. Annie had made ginger-bread, and the air in the house was laced with the smell of cinnamon and nutmeg. She piled biscuits on to a plate for them to take upstairs, still hot from the oven.

'Behave yourselves,' she said brightly, as they left the room.

'Do you tell your mum *everything*?' Sal asked, when they'd climbed the two sets of stairs to the attic and reached Pax's room. It was impeccably tidy. The bed had been neatly made and was piled high with cushions. Aloysius was out, roaming the floor in a large turquoise exercise ball.

Sal tried imagining sitting his own mother down and telling her about his love life. The idea felt laughable. In fact, he couldn't remember the last time he had told her *anything* about himself.

'Of course not,' Pax said. 'Just most things.'

'Like who you've been snogging,' Sal said grumpily. He threw himself on to the bed, making himself at home among the plush cushions and knitted blankets, and stuffed one of the gingerbread biscuits into his mouth.

'I hadn't kissed anyone before,' Pax protested, sitting on the furry beanbag opposite. He pulled his knees into his chest and stared beseechingly at him. 'It was a big moment.'

Sal took the biscuit back out of his mouth and set it back on the plate. He cleared his throat. 'You hadn't kissed anyone before?'

Pax sighed. 'You're the first person who's let me.'

'I don't know what I was thinking,' Sal teased.

Pax got off the beanbag and joined him on the bed. He knelt in front of him, placed his hands on his shoulders and leant in pointedly. 'Do you like me?'

'I like you,' Sal said. He meant it. But the words came out sounding tight and snappy.

Pax raised his eyebrows.

'I like you,' Sal tried again. 'I like you a lot. Don't look at me like that.'

'How should I look at you?'

He lifted his hands to cover Pax's eyes. He could feel his eyelashes brushing against his skin. 'You shouldn't.'

'But I like looking at you.'

'Do you like kissing me?'

Pax laughed and tried to pull Sal's hands away from his eyes. 'I like that too.'

Sal moved a hand to the back of his neck. 'Then close your eyes.'

It felt inevitable that Sal was going to kiss him again, sooner or later. So he did it, and Pax moaned against his mouth, back arching as he pressed himself forward against him. It made Sal's stomach roll in a hot, twisting way that was, actually, uncomfortable. He frowned and pulled away, wondering if that was going to happen every time they kissed and, if so, exactly how he was going to live with it.

'Sorry,' Pax said, meeting his eye and looking mortified. 'Am I not any good at it?'

'Actually,' Sal said, 'you're a bit *too* good at it.'

Pax laughed at that. He wriggled backwards, putting space between them. 'How are things at your house?' he asked. 'Any luck with the lavender?'

Sal made a non-committal grumbling sound. Pax hadn't asked about his house in days, and he'd thought they might have been able to let the subject drop.

'Should we try more sage?' Pax pressed.

'I don't know,' Sal said. 'I don't know if anything like that will make a difference.'

'But we won't know unless we keep trying,' Pax said. 'I don't understand why you don't want to talk about it.'

'Maybe I don't like sharing your attention with the undead,' Sal said, quirking an eyebrow. He laced his fingers through Pax's and only felt marginally guilty when Pax's expression of frustration melted into one of contentment.

Pax leant in closer. 'I could forgive you for that.'

'Dirk thinks this is hilarious,' Sal told him, gesturing down at their intertwined hands.

Pax pulled a face of pure confusion. 'Dirk is weird.'

'He'd say the same about you.'

Pax made a thoughtful humming noise. 'And what do you think?'

'I think you're *both* nuts,' Sal said. 'And I'm totally normal.'

Pax gripped his hand tighter, squeezing his fingers. '*This* feels normal.'

'Yeah,' Sal said. He squeezed back, surprised at the realization that Pax was right. 'This feels really normal.'

Night had fallen by the time Sal left. Pax had forced him to watch a show about werewolves, and it had turned out to be so good that they had finished half the first series before it occurred to Sal that it might be time to leave. Outside the sky had turned pitch-black, and it had started to rain. There was an owl hooting somewhere in the distance.

There were an awkward few seconds outside Pax's

front door, where they both hesitated over whether or not to kiss goodbye and accidentally bumped noses when they both moved in at the same time. When Pax disappeared back inside the house, Sal could hear him let out a whoop of excitement from the other side of the front door.

CHAPTER TWENTY-ONE

At school, not much changed. To Sal's surprise, nobody looked twice if Pax grabbed his hand in the middle of the corridors. Which he did frequently, without any apparent sense of embarrassment. Dirk snorted with laughter when Sal mentioned this.

'That's because everyone thought you were already doing it,' he told him bluntly. 'After you turned Jo down at the Halloween party.' Then he frowned. 'Apart from me. And now I owe Elsie ten quid. I thought you were straight.'

'Yeah, well,' Sal said, shrugging. 'So did I.'

It hadn't been much of a revelation, and he had been surprised to find he didn't really care. It explained why he had never enjoyed kissing girls much, which was helpful. Otherwise, it made no real difference to him and he didn't see the point in pretending otherwise.

'What does Asha think?' Dirk asked. This was his favourite question in any conversation, whether Sal was failing his exams, or trying to decide what to have for dinner.

'She doesn't know.'

'Oh,' Dirk said. 'Shit.'

'Yeah.'

'She'll be cool with it,' he said, voice full of confidence. His eyes took on the wistful expression that Sal was all too familiar with. 'She likes Pax, right?'

Sal mumbled something incoherent and Dirk fixed him with a glare.

'You've gotta tell her.'

'Yeah,' Sal said. There was no point in arguing with Dirk where Asha was concerned. 'I'll tell her tonight.'

Sal had no intention of telling Asha. Just the thought of doing so made him nervous. He wasn't entirely sure how she felt about Pax, but got the impression she didn't like how much time they were spending together. He had stopped talking about him in front of her, and was making an effort to keep Pax away from the house.

Dirk, for once, had the tact to change the subject.

'I've got my driving test on Wednesday,' he told him. 'Third time lucky. I think I'm gonna smash it this time.'

Sal snorted. 'You'll smash something,' he said.

Dirk had turned seventeen six months before and had been trying to pass his driving test ever since. He had failed his first by hitting a lamp post, and his second by driving into a ditch.

Most days, after school, Sal went back to Pax's house. Pax still didn't seem to mind when Sal didn't have much to say in response to his constant chattering. Only now, Pax used his silences as opportunities to kiss him, meaning they both forgot what they had been saying and frequently had to restart conversations from the beginning.

Pax's mother's Keep the Door Open rule was also becoming increasingly frustrating. The woman appeared as if by magic whenever they dared to close it, offering them milk and cookies before disappearing with the door left wide open in her wake. She still ruffled Sal's hair whenever he left the house. But she did it slightly too hard, fixing him with a steely gaze as she did so.

Sal quickly discovered that he wasn't very good at romance. He never knew what Pax was thinking or when he wanted him to take his hand, or when he wanted to be kissed.

Luckily Pax provided a running commentary of what was going on in his head most of the time. Within a week of having kissed him Sal knew everything about him, from why his Uncle Wilfred had moved to Scotland to exactly how he liked Sal's fingers to move through his hair.

The more he got to know Pax, though, the more the boy seemed to expect in return. Sal refusing to offer information on his life didn't stop Pax attempting to find out about it.

'I've been thinking,' Pax said on a Sunday in mid-November. It was a rainy afternoon and they were spending it curled up in his room.

'Oh no,' Sal said. He set down the book he had been reading. It was a battered old copy of one of Pax's vampire romances. He had picked it up as a joke and was enjoying it more than he really wanted to let on. The main character was just about to get bitten. 'About what?'

'About what you said,' Pax told him. 'About your mum thinking your dad is still with you. Still in the house.'

'What about it?' Sal asked. It sounded ridiculous, when Pax put it like that. He wished he hadn't said anything at all.

'Well,' Pax continued. 'Do you still see him? Do you . . . see his ghost?'

Sal shook his head. 'It's not really like that.'

'Then what's it like?'

'It's hard to explain,' Sal said.

Pax looked frustrated. 'You won't ever talk to me about it.'

Sal scowled at him. 'I don't *want* to talk about it. I've told you that before.'

'Then how am I supposed to help?' Pax asked. He sat down next to Sal and poked him in the ribs.

'I didn't ask you to help,' Sal pointed out.

'But I feel like I should.'

Sal shook his head and pulled him close. He tried kissing him to distract him and managed to keep him quiet for ten blissful seconds before Pax wriggled free.

'Why do we never go to your house any more?' he asked.

Sal resisted the urge to point out that he had never actually *invited* Pax to his house. The boy just turned up. Repeatedly.

'I like your house better,' he said, catching Pax's hand and playing with his fingers. He pressed a kiss to the soft pad of each in turn and Pax started blushing but shook him off.

'You're not telling me something.' He reached over and rapped Sal on the head with his knuckles, as if knocking at a closed door. 'Let me in.'

Sal looked away. 'I'm not,' he said. 'I mean, *I am.*'

'It's your mum, isn't it?'

Sal pulled back, a creeping feeling of dread rising inside him. He had been so careful to keep the truth a secret, convinced it would tear everything apart.

'What do you mean?' he asked, voice cold.

'Nothing,' Pax said, recoiling at the bite in Sal's voice. 'But you won't let me near her. Are you ashamed of me? Do you think I'm going to embarrass you?'

He was rambling, cheeks turning redder. There were tears brewing in his eyes and Sal's stomach turned at the sight of them.

'No,' he said. 'No, of course not.'

Sal supposed he shouldn't have been surprised that Pax had noticed he'd been keeping him away from his house. Pax was surprisingly observant, even if he did seem to be living in another world half of the time.

'You've met *my* mum,' Pax said.

But Annie was normal, Sal thought. She cared about

things like the fruit to pastry ratio in her apple pies, and her son's exam results, and who he was letting into his bedroom. Sal's mother was many things. But she certainly wasn't ordinary.

'My mum's different,' he said shortly.

'Dirk's met her,' Pax continued, wounded. He looked down at his own hands, where he had started picking at the embroidery of one of his cushions. 'He knows you better than I do.'

'Oh god.' Sal stared at him in horror. He didn't like the expression on Pax's face. 'You don't think I'm into *Dirk*, do you?'

Pax still wasn't meeting his eye. 'He's your best friend. And he has footballer legs.'

'Exactly,' Sal said. 'He's a friend. You're my— Hang on, why are you looking at Dirk's legs?'

'I'm your *what*?' Pax asked, looking a good deal more focused than Sal was accustomed to.

'Um,' Sal mumbled. 'My . . . I dunno . . . my boyfriend? Maybe. If you wanted. Not if you didn't. Obviously.'

Pax looked as if he might be about to pass out from excitement. He grabbed Sal's face between his hands and kissed him abruptly on the nose. 'I've never had a boyfriend before.'

'Yeah,' Sal said, grinning. 'It shows.'

Pax laughed and Sal lifted a hand to tilt his face and get in closer. Things were just beginning to get interesting when Pax wriggled out of his grip and stood up. Sal sat up straight and watched him go. He crossed the room, closed the door silently and jumped back on to the bed, climbing awkwardly into Sal's lap.

'Oh,' Sal mumbled, as Pax began an assault on his mouth. 'Yeah, OK.'

He wasn't used to wanting to touch people. Mostly he just wanted everyone to keep their distance . . . but not Pax. He wanted Pax as close as he could possibly get him.

He pushed his hands cautiously under his fluffy jumper and Pax squirmed on top of him, his warm breath turning into a giggle against his neck.

'You're cute,' Sal said, pulling him closer, his hands brushing bare skin.

'You're tickling me,' Pax said, giggling again as Sal's hands ran up his waist.

Sal held him tighter. His heart was beating so quickly he could barely breathe. All he could think about was the bright electric shock of Pax's touch.

'I like you so much.'

Pax stopped giggling. His eyes darkened and he leant in and kissed Sal again. Their teeth clashed together and his hands slipped under Sal's T-shirt and slid over his chest. Sal was just contemplating pulling Pax's jumper up over his head when they were interrupted by a furious knocking at the door.

'PAX,' Annie shouted from behind it. '*Door!*'

Pax startled and rolled off him. Sal groaned and pressed the heels of his hands into his eyes. Aloysius the hamster was watching them with a disdainful expression from across the room.

Annie knocked again and pushed the door open. She poked her head around and regarded them both with narrowed eyes. Sal drew his knees up to his chest and nervously tried to tame his wildly tousled hair.

'Cup of tea in the kitchen?' she asked in a tone that made it perfectly clear it was not a suggestion.

'OK,' Pax said mournfully. He wiped his mouth on the back of his hand. 'We'll be down in a minute.'

She nodded and turned her back, shooting Sal a distrustful look over her shoulder before she went.

'*I* won't. I'm leaving,' Sal said, mortified, as soon as she had disappeared down the stairs. He scrambled off the bed and searched the room for his hoodie.

'You can't,' Pax protested.

'I'm not sitting and drinking tea with your mum when she knows I've just had my tongue in your mouth.'

'I think she thinks you do most of the time,' Pax said.

'Oh god,' Sal said. He pulled on his trainers and tugged the laces into rough, hurried knots. 'Well, now I'm definitely leaving.'

CHAPTER TWENTY-TWO

The morning after his driving test, Dirk arrived at Sal's house in his father's beaten-up Volvo, despite living less than a ten-minute walk away. Sal stuck his head out of the window at the sound of the horn beeping. Dirk had parked at the end of the drive, just outside the gate. He waved out of the window at him, grinning.

'Get in,' he shouted, when Sal had opened the front door. 'We're going on an adventure.'

'It's a school day,' Sal said, as he reached the end of the drive. He vaulted the gate and leant down to look in the passenger-side window. 'Where are we going?'

'We are *going*,' Dirk rapped out a drum roll against his own legs, 'to the beach.'

Elsie, it transpired, was already sitting in the back seat of the car, flicking through a magazine and dressed for a cold day's walk. Sal raced inside again, ditched his backpack and rummaged through his wardrobe for the thickest hoodie he owned. He helped himself to two crisp twenty-pound notes from the cookie jar in the kitchen before jogging back down the drive and jumping into the passenger seat. Two minutes later, they stopped to pick up Pax on his way down the lane.

'Get in, loser,' Dirk said, performing an emergency stop and sticking his head out of the window. 'We're going shopping.'

'Oh, I love *Mean Girls*,' Pax said as he approached the car. 'We should all watch it together. That would be fun.' He hesitated with his hand on the door handle. 'We're not actually going shopping, though, are we?'

'Nah,' Dirk said. 'We're going to the beach.'

'But what about school?' Pax asked, climbing into the back next to Elsie and looking around doubtfully at the peeling leather seats and dusty dashboard. He sniffed cautiously. The car smelt strongly of petrol, wet dog and Werther's Originals. 'Won't we get into trouble?'

''Course not,' Dirk said, pulling away down the lane in a screech of wheelspin and flying gravel. One of Mrs Helliwell's tabby cats hissed and arched its back as they passed. 'It'll be educational. Think of it as a field trip.'

Elsie snorted in disbelief. 'How will it be educational?'

'I don't know,' Dirk grumbled. 'Christ. We'll find some fossils or something.'

Sal turned around in his seat to grin at Pax, and the doubt fell away from his expression. Pax beamed back, unzipped his coat and unwrapped his scarf, settling into the seat. Sal wondered if he should feel guilty for being a bad influence, but decided it would do him good. Pax had perfect grades anyway, despite having started a full month behind everyone else.

'Should we play I Spy?' Pax suggested, an hour into the journey.

'No,' Sal, Dirk and Elsie said, in perfect unison.

Pax began playing anyway and, for lack of anything better to do, the three of them ended up joining in. They spent half an hour trying to guess Pax's something beginning with S, before it turned out to be a *speck of dust*. After that, no one had the energy to continue.

It took two hours to reach the coast and crawl down the tiny country lanes that led to the beach. As they drew closer, the sea appeared and disappeared behind the hills on the horizon, and the sun finally succeeded in breaking through the clouds.

They parked in a seafront car park in a dreary village, which smelt of fish and seemed to consist of little more than a scattering of houses, a cafe and a church. They ran together over the grassy dunes and down on to the beach. The air was fresher on the sand, a cold wind being whipped in on the waves, bringing the scent of salt and the tang of seaweed.

Dirk and Pax found an old rowing boat, rotting away on the sand. They climbed inside immediately and sat down on its tiny wooden benches. Sal followed Elsie towards the sea. She had barely said a word on the drive, despite Dirk's frequent attempts to tease her.

'Are you OK?' he asked, when she finally drew to a halt.

'Yes,' she said. She grinned suddenly. 'You and Pax are cute together.'

'Shut up,' Sal said.

Elsie did shut up, and he began to feel bad for telling her to. She was staring out at the horizon, a distant expression on her face.

'Do you miss Jacob?' he asked.

'Yeah,' she said. 'Do you think that's stupid?'

'No. I'm glad you broke up with him, though. You were too good for him.'

'I want you to know,' she said, slowly, as if she wasn't really sure she wanted to say anything at all. 'About Jacob . . .'

She trailed off. Sal tried to look politely confused. He had heard what had happened with Jacob – the entire school had. But he still wished he hadn't; he felt like he had stolen a part of Elsie's life that should have only belonged to her.

'Nothing happened,' Elsie said. She twisted her hands together and stared back out to sea, as if suddenly afraid to meet Sal's eye.

'Oh,' Sal said. 'Yeah, OK.'

'No,' Elsie said abruptly. '*Really*. Nothing happened. We didn't do anything. He wanted to, but I wasn't ready.'

'But that's great!' Sal clapped her on the back, relieved for her. 'You really can do better.'

She was still staring straight ahead, mouth set in a very tight line, jaw clenched.

Sal frowned. 'Why are you letting him lie about it, though?'

'I don't know,' Elsie said. 'My friends always thought I was being stupid, when I said I wasn't ready, so I just . . .'

'Let them think he was telling the truth?'

'And now everyone's saying I'm a slut.' Elsie shrugged. She kicked at the shell-strewn sand beneath her feet. 'I literally *cannot* win.'

'So tell everyone he's lying,' Sal said.

'Nobody would believe me.' Elsie turned her back on him, and reached down to pick up one of the shells she'd crushed beneath her shoes. She crunched her hand into a fist around it and reopened it, letting the tiny particles fall through her fingers back to the ground. 'Anyway. That's not the point.'

Sal fell silent for a minute, realizing he'd said the wrong thing, and not quite knowing how to put it right.

'Would you like me to break his nose?' he offered. He cracked his knuckles in a weak attempt to cheer her up.

'What?' she said, finally smiling. 'You think I can't do that myself?'

'You know . . .' Sal reached out and wrapped an arm around her shoulders. 'He really is an idiot.'

'You're lucky,' Elsie said, and Sal could tell she wanted to change the subject. 'Having Pax.'

'I know.'

'He's good for you. He makes you happier.'

'Yeah,' Sal said. Pax could make him smile even when he didn't want to. And did, frequently. 'He's annoying like that.'

They were interrupted by Pax and Dirk running up behind them and throwing themselves at their backs, Dirk with such force that Elsie staggered forward into the surf. Pax landed with his legs around Sal's waist and his hands on his head. Sal attempted to shake him off, turning around to shout at Dirk, but caught a glimpse of Elsie laughing as he attempted to wrestle her into the sea. The pained look had left her eyes, and her face was lit up in the weak autumn sunlight. He wasn't sure if she was crying, or if the spray from the waves had hit her face.

Pax laughed in his ear, still clinging to his back. He felt feather-light. Sal gripped hold of his legs, still clamped around his waist. He turned around and raced down the beach with him, until Pax was squealing with laughter and begging him to stop.

When he turned around, Elsie had won the wrestling match through pure tenacity and Dirk had fallen face first into the surf. She was doubled over with laughter, ankle-deep in the waves. Pax toppled off Sal's back and staggered down the beach towards them.

Sal launched himself forward, reaching out to grab him, and Pax turned and sprinted away from him across the sand, the pom-poms on his scarf flying out in the wind behind him.

He wasn't a particularly fast runner (all legs, but no power) but Sal let him get away for the simple pleasure of

172

prolonging the chase. When they reached the others, Elsie was still laughing and Dirk was shivering violently, his jeans and T-shirt soaked through to the skin.

The four of them knelt at the edge of the water and built a sandcastle, until the icy damp burnt their knees and their hands were motionless with the cold. Then they stood and watched as the waves came in and it crumbled and was washed cleanly away.

The sun was lying low in the sky when they finally walked back up the beach, feet sinking into the damp sand. On the promenade they stopped at a scruffy cafe with blue vinyl seats and lobster nets hanging from the ceiling. Dirk spent ten minutes standing under the hand dryer in the bathroom, drying his jeans. They ordered chips for everyone in his absence, which arrived steaming hot and crusted with salt. Pax had ordered a hot chocolate with marshmallows and, ignoring their horror, he proceeded to dunk his chips into his mug.

'Don't think I'm kissing you after you've eaten that,' Sal said, and Pax just smiled at him, because they both knew that he still would.

He dunked another chip into his mug and leant across the table, holding it up to Sal's mouth in silent challenge.

Unable to resist a dare, Sal wrinkled up his nose, and bit the chip in two. It was the perfect blend of salty and sweet, and it disappeared, cloud-like, in his mouth. He swallowed.

'See?' Pax said. 'It's good, isn't it?'

Sal grinned and leant in, biting the rest of the chip out from between his fingers. 'It could be worse.'

Elsie and Dirk were pulling matching faces of disgust on the other side of the table. Sal's ears were still burning from the cold, and Pax's nose had turned a delicate shade of rosy pink. In the car on the way home, they shared the back seat and Pax sat in the middle, where he fell asleep against Sal's shoulder.

It was a perfect day.

CHAPTER TWENTY-THREE

The problem with perfect days is that the universe always finds a way to collect its debt.

They dropped Pax off at home first and he squeezed Sal's hand before getting out of the car. Two minutes later, they pulled up at the end of Sal's drive, just in time to see Asha returning from work at the *Herald*. She disappeared through the front door, still dressed in her suit jacket, and carrying half a dozen straining shopping bags in her hands. Lulled into a sleepy state of contentment by the sea air, the huge portion of chips and the motion of the car, Sal made the mistake of letting Dirk hop out of the car and follow her inside.

He lingered behind, not wanting the day to end. Elsie was snoring softly in the passenger seat and she grumbled and batted him away when he leant forward to try to shake her awake. He left her sleeping and followed Dirk into the house.

Sal pulled off his sand-crusted trainers at the front door, yawned widely and followed the sound of voices through to the kitchen. Dirk was enthusiastically helping Asha with the shopping, piling things out of bags and examining them as if they might give him some kind of an insight into her soul.

She seemed unusually cheerful and was tolerating Dirk's clumsy attempts at helping her. She had even turned on the radio, which normally she said she couldn't stand. When Sal walked in, she looked up and smiled nervously.

'Sal, I need to talk to you.'

She glanced at Dirk, as if expecting him to take the hint and leave them in peace. He continued to stack tins in the wrong cupboard, half turning to listen more carefully to whatever Asha was about to say.

'Later, then,' Asha said. She looked Sal up and down. 'Why are you covered in sand?'

Sal looked down at the floor to see they had trailed a stream of sand into the kitchen. The ends of his jeans were crusted with it and still damp from the sea.

'We went to the beach,' Dirk said chirpily.

One of Sal's favourite things about Asha was that she hardly ever tried to tell him what to do. She let him make his own decisions and ribbed him about them afterwards.

'Oh, great,' she said, voice dripping with sarcasm. She was on tiptoe, pushing bags of crisps and pasta into the cupboards. 'Why bother going to school when you can just swan off and do your own thing?'

'Exactly,' Dirk said. 'You should have come. Now that Sal and Pax are an item, we could double-date.'

Sal froze in place. His heart felt as if it had flown up into his throat. Asha dropped the packet of pasta she had been holding. The plastic split and tubes of macaroni went skittering across the floor. When she turned to face Sal, her expression had turned to ice.

'Oh, shit,' Dirk said, hands faltering on a tin of beans. 'You didn't know, did you?'

She didn't bother turning back to face him. Her eyes were narrowed and fixed on Sal in stony disapproval.

'Bye, Dirk,' she said.

Dirk turned to look pleadingly at Sal. 'You said you were gonna tell her.'

Sal shook his head and pointed him towards the door. 'Just . . . go.'

Dirk left them in an icy silence. Asha continued to stare at him, and Sal half turned away, picking up a carton of fresh orange juice that Dirk had left on the kitchen table.

'Why didn't you tell me?' Asha asked.

'Look,' Sal said. He took a swig of juice, straight from the carton, in the hope it would wash his heart out of his throat and back down to his chest where it belonged. 'Who I'm dating isn't any of your business.'

It wasn't the right thing to say. Asha looked even more annoyed than she had before he had spoken. Sal turned around and started down the hall. He brought the orange juice with him and took another gulp out of the carton in an attempt to look casual.

'I don't care that you're dating him, you idiot,' Asha said, following him. 'A blindfolded bat could've seen that you fancied him.'

'Well, what's the problem?' Sal asked, irritated. He hadn't thought it had been that obvious. In fact, he'd spent the past month working it out. 'I thought you liked him.'

'I *do* like him,' she growled, looking like she didn't particularly like anyone right then. 'I just don't like the games he's got you playing.'

'What games?'

'Lavender wreaths, crystals . . .' She moved to stand in front of him, forcing him to meet her eye. '*Setting things on fire.*'

'They're not games,' Sal said. 'He's trying to help.'

He tried to push past her and she fell back but grabbed him by his T-shirt as he made for the stairs. He wrenched it out of her grip and shoved her away.

'Get off me,' he said. '*What* is your problem?'

'My problem,' she snapped, 'is that he's got you thinking that craft projects and pretty stones are going to make things better. They're not.'

'At least he's trying.'

Asha's eyes narrowed. 'What's that supposed to mean?'

Sal turned his back on her and retreated up the stairs.

They didn't speak to each other for the rest of the evening. In the mood to be alone, Sal stayed in his bedroom. Night fell, and he could smell Asha frying quesadillas in the kitchen. She only cooked when she was unhappy, so Sal figured she was still angry and stayed well away. His stomach was grumbling when he finally crawled under the covers of his bed.

CHAPTER TWENTY-FOUR

The next morning, Sal awoke to find dark circles had appeared under his eyes. He had slept fitfully and was running late for school.

When Asha yelled up the stairs to tell him Dirk was outside, he stuck his head out of the window and shouted that he would follow him. He didn't want to walk with him anyway. He hadn't forgiven him for letting slip to Asha about Pax.

It was grey and gloomy when he stepped outside, as if someone had forgotten to tell the sky it was morning. He had layered one hoodie over another and lifted both hoods over his head as he left the house, shielding his face against the cold. Pax had lent him one of his many pairs of gloves, and he pulled them on as he walked down the drive, the wool soft and fuzzy against his skin.

When he arrived at school the bell had already rung, but it seemed to have had even less of an effect than usual. There was a large crowd of people still gathered around the entrance, and yet more dotted around in groups around the grounds, their heads bowed against the cold.

Sal passed the stragglers and pushed through the crowd at the main entrance. He was halfway down the corridor when he caught sight of Pax hurtling towards him. He was holding a copy of a newspaper, and nearly fell down the steps in his rush to reach him.

'Hey,' Sal said, stopping and grinning at the sight of Pax running. He reached a hand out to him but instead of taking it, Pax shoved the paper into it. He gestured down at it, out of breath and seemingly unable to speak.

Sal looked down and his heart skipped a beat.

The groups of stragglers suddenly made sense. They weren't bowing their heads against the cold at all. They were reading.

It was the *Holden Herald* and emblazoned across the front page was yet another photograph of his house. This time, the doors were flung open and the dusty chandelier and decaying staircase were visible beyond. Beneath the photo, in thick black lettering, were the words: *Life in a 'Haunted' House*.

Sal stared down at it, his stomach rolling over. He couldn't tear his eyes away from the headline. Two minuscule black marks were filling him with dread. Why had *Haunted* been printed in quotation marks?

He didn't think he could bear to read any further.

Then, his eyes dropped involuntarily to the next line of text. His heart lurched. In miniature, cramped italics was the author's name.

ASHA ROSE AMANI.

He read the first line of the article.

Let me tell you what it's like to be haunted.

Horrified, Sal's eyes dropped to the final few paragraphs. The ink was scuffed, and the paper crumpled from where Pax had been clutching it. Sal knew, before he had even started reading, that what was written there was going to change everything.

When the light turns on, the ghost disappears. That's the reality of living in a haunted house. Ghosts are made up of memories, and amplified by darkness. The honest truth is a simple one: ghosts aren't real. But, for some people, the idea can become not something to be scared of, but something to cling on to.

My father died five years ago, leaving me, my mother and brother behind. Death hits differently when you live in a haunted house. You can't help hoping the person you've lost isn't really gone. For my brother and me, that hope soon faded. But not for our mother. She had always believed in ghosts.

For years, she lived a half-life. She was never a hundred per cent with us, preoccupied with the idea that our father's spirit lingered on in the house. She convinced herself she could hear his voice when the lights went out. That sometimes, she could feel the imprint of his body in the bed next to her.

As the years went on, the illusion began to fade, and she was angry: at the house because it couldn't ever really bring him back. And at my brother and me, for not believing.

Two months ago, she left for good, leaving us, both still teenagers, alone in the house. Her absence is a secret we've been hiding ever since, scared that if anyone found out then what remained of our family might be torn apart.

CHAPTER TWENTY-FIVE

'I'm going,' Sal said. He felt sick with rage, his heart pounding in his chest. When he looked up, he felt like he was seeing through a haze. Pax's face swam before him, blurred and pale.

'But . . .' Pax said, as though from very far away. 'You've only just arrived.'

Sal ignored him. The only thing that mattered was finding Asha and confronting her with what she had done. He tore the article from the paper and clenched it tightly in his fist. Somewhere in the background, the school bell rang again, its shrill peal a distant whistle in Sal's mind. On either side of him, students were jostling past, turning to look at him as they went. Some slapped him encouragingly on the back. Most kept a wide berth, passing in packs and lowering their voices to whisper to their friends.

Sal turned around. He pushed back against the current, slamming backpacks and bodies out of his way as he went. He elbowed past Elsie, who squawked in indignation and shoved him straight back. Mr Gulliver appeared from his office as he passed it. He called Sal's name, and Sal kept walking. He walked straight past him, and back towards the wide-open doors at the end of the corridor. The autumn sunlight was streaming in through them, and he broke into a jog as he neared them, then burst through at a sprint.

Far behind him, Pax was calling for him to come back. His voice was little more than a whisper on the wind.

Sal ran over the sodden playing fields, cold air whistling past his ears, and down through the woods where the branches caught on his clothes as he passed. Then on to Yew Tree Lane, where with each breathless step, he beat his anger out into the ground at his feet. His footsteps reverberated like the thudding of clock hands, like the tapping of a drum.

He jumped the gate and flew down the drive, barrelling through the front door seconds later. Asha was drying dishes in the kitchen. She turned around when he entered, and her expression of confusion changed to one of alarm when he slammed the newspaper article down on the kitchen table before her.

'It was supposed to be next week,' she said, reaching a faltering hand out to hold it. Her fingertips hovered over the print as if it were something very precious that she didn't quite dare to touch, and landed over her own name.

'They told me next week.'

'You *sold* this?' Sal grabbed it back out of her reach and brandished it at her. 'You *sold* this shit?'

'No,' Asha protested. 'It's for my internship. They're not paying me. I didn't do it for *money*, Sal.'

'Then what did you do it for, Asha?'

Asha twisted the tea towel between her hands.

'They were going to run another article anyway,' she said. 'That reporter, Faris Jones, he wouldn't let it go. He kept asking me questions about the house. And about Dad. I just wanted to tell it my own way.'

It suddenly became clear to Sal exactly what Asha had been doing all those evenings, curled up with her laptop, fingers racing over the keys. She had been gearing up to this for weeks, writing and rewriting a story that wasn't even hers to tell. Threading together the words she would use to tear his life apart.

'I wanted to write something real,' Asha pushed on, voice pleading. 'And once I'd started writing about it, I couldn't stop. I wanted . . . I wanted people to *know*. I can't keep this secret any more, Salem.'

Sal's anger was so sharp it was sickening. His head throbbed with thick, foggy hatred. Asha was blurring in front of his eyes.

'It's not *your* secret to tell,' he spat.

'I was going to tell you,' Asha protested, the tea towel a tense coil in her hands. 'I *swear* I was going to tell you. They said it wouldn't run until next week.'

'Yeah, well. Looks like it was a slow news day,' Sal said.

'You've turned our entire lives into a scrap of gossip in the local paper. Congratulations.'

'It's not gossip, Salem. It's the truth.' There was a deep ruby flush spreading up Asha's neck. A vein throbbing in her temple. She folded her arms, drawing herself up to her full height. All five foot of it. 'That's what journalism is.'

Sal snorted, the sound tearing out of his throat before he could stop it. 'You're not a journalist.'

'I could be,' Asha shouted, nostrils flaring. 'You think I want to work in the local shop for the rest of my life? I don't just want to sit and rot here, Salem.'

'Well, you're going to,' Sal said. Every ounce of bitterness he had ever felt came pouring out into his words. They were both going to. 'So get fucking used to it.'

They were interrupted by a soft tapping at the door. Sal whirled around and stormed down the hall to answer it, leaving Asha apoplectic with rage behind him. She slammed the kitchen door so hard the entire hall shook and dust descended from the ceiling.

It was Pax at the front door. His eyes were wide with concern and his cheeks were red from running and for a second Sal felt his anger pull away. Then Pax stepped forward and Sal spotted another copy of the paper clutched in his hands. He wondered how many he could burn and realized it wouldn't ever be enough.

'I don't understand,' Pax said, gesturing breathlessly at the paper, his words coming out in great ragged gasps. 'Asha's article says the house isn't haunted.'

He was looking at Sal as if he thought this perfectly

reasonable assertion, printed in black and white, could not possibly be true and he was still waiting for him to correct it. From the kitchen came the sound of breaking glass, and Asha swearing at the top of her voice. Sal stepped outside on to the porch, pushing Pax back and closing the door behind them.

'Salem?' Pax's face fell into a frown. He was visibly twitching with the urge to get through the door. 'She said your mum left you both. That the haunting was just in her head.'

Sal didn't say anything, and Pax's expression crumpled. He wrapped his arms around his chest, shivering in the autumn chill.

'You didn't tell me.'

Sal pointed down at the newspaper between them. The very sight of it was making his stomach turn. 'You read it,' he said, voice raw.

Pax looked confused. He looked down at the paper in his hand. He was gripping it so tightly that the ink had blurred, and grey stains darkened his fingers. 'Of course I did.'

'You had no right to read that.'

'But . . . everyone's read it, Salem. It's in the newspaper.'

'So?' Sal barked. 'It's none of your business. You think you have some kind of a right to my secrets?'

'No,' Pax said. He recoiled at the anger in Sal's words. 'I just thought you'd *want* to share them with me. I thought you already had. You could have told me, Salem.'

'We don't *tell* people,' Sal snapped. He turned to stare

out down the drive, lifting his hands to his eyes and pushing back the tears that were threatening to spill out. '*Fuck.*'

'This whole time . . .' Pax twisted his hands together in what looked like a painful contortion, crumpling the newspaper between them, turning the black and white to grey pulp. 'This whole time, I thought we were being honest with each other. You let me think it was all real . . . that the house was haunted. That your mum was right here. How could you do that to me?'

'I didn't.' Sal folded his arms across his chest. 'It was what you wanted to think.'

'What?'

'You thought it was fun,' Sal said. His throat felt horribly tight and his voice came out sounding harsher than he intended. 'And exciting, and . . . I don't know, romantic. Well, it isn't. Life isn't. And it's not my problem if you can't deal with that.'

Pax bit his lip. His mouth was set in a firm, straight line, jaw clenched. 'How was I supposed to know you were lying to me?'

Sal rolled his eyes, still fighting back the tears threatening to fill them. 'Ghosts aren't real, Pax. Grow up.'

Pax spun away from him. He walked down the front steps and, when he turned back to look at him, his face had hardened, eyes turning steely in a way Sal would not have thought possible. He would never have guessed it would be possible for him to feel scared of Pax. The idea was laughable. But for a passing second, for one frozen moment, he did.

'I didn't care about the ghosts, Salem. I cared about you.'

He walked away down the drive, glancing over his shoulder just once, as if expecting to be followed. Sal watched him go. His thudding chest felt empty. His throat felt full. His voice wasn't working, and he didn't call him back.

He waited until Pax had disappeared over the gate. Then he slammed his fist into the front door. Hard enough to make it creak and shake. The wood splintered under his knuckles and when he lifted them to his face, they were beaded with blood.

He sank down on to the front steps, and sat there for what seemed like hours, blinking into the autumn sunlight and waiting for Pax to come back.

CHAPTER TWENTY-SIX

By the time Sal went back inside, his hands and feet had turned numb. The pounding in his head had dulled too, and his anger had seeped away into the cold air. Instead, he felt very empty. The phone was ringing and nobody was bothering to answer it.

Asha was sitting waiting at the top of the stairs, resting her elbows on her knees and with her head cupped in her hands. She frowned down at him, worrying her lip between her teeth.

'Mum's gonna kill you,' Sal said. 'When she finds out.'

Asha folded her arms across her chest. 'You're assuming she's going to come back.'

'She will,' Sal snapped. 'Of course she will.'

'It's been two months, Sal,' Asha said, her tone softening. 'And there's been barely a word.'

They had heard from her only once since she had left. A text message, sent two days after she'd left, when Asha had begun to worry and threatened to go to the police. It had said that she was safe, and would be back soon, and that she just needed some time. Sal and Asha had thought *some time* meant a few days, and then a few weeks. By the time it occurred to them that *some time* might actually mean for ever, she had been gone two months.

Sal leant back against the door and closed his eyes, willing Asha away. When he opened them, he was confronted with the sight of the lavender wreath, still hanging from the coat hooks by the door. It was starting to disintegrate, the purple flowers turning a dull shade of silver. He tore it from the coat hook and crushed it in his fist. It crumbled to a pale grey dust.

Asha stood up and made her way down towards him, the wooden stairs creaking beneath her feet. The phone rang off and immediately started again. Mr Gulliver, Sal assumed. He had probably read the article by now and would have recognized Asha's name at the top. He had probably worked out that it was Asha who had answered the phone when Sal had been suspended. He would know that their mum had left them. Everybody would. The thought made Sal even more furious.

'I can't believe you did it,' he said. He stared at her, unable to fathom the depths of her betrayal. 'You said we couldn't say anything.'

Their mother's absence was something they never

talked about. Not even with each other. Silence was the only tool they had to keep themselves safe – to keep the remnants of their family together. For weeks they had lived in fear of someone finding out they were alone in the house. They hadn't known what might happen. If social services might be called. Or the police. If they would have to leave, and go and live somewhere else. If people would pity them, or worse, think they had driven their own mother away.

They were, both of them, living half under the pretence that she was still there. Neither one of them had turned off the radio she had left blaring in the studio upstairs. It played day and night, through unspoken agreement. She had left an empty coffee pot on the kitchen countertop, which they'd left untouched. It was long dried up – its insides black and crusting.

Sal had closed her bedroom door the day after she left, and neither of them had been inside since. She had packed a bag before she'd left, and Sal didn't want to know what she had chosen to take, and what – like them – she had deemed dispensable enough to leave behind.

At the bottom of the stairs, Asha folded her arms and stood her ground. Her dark stormy scowl was a perfect mirror of Sal's own.

'I'm nearly eighteen now,' she said. 'We're safe.'

'Pax has read it. We—' Sal's voice cracked. He cleared his throat. 'It's all your fault.'

Asha hesitated, her frown faltering.

'You'll make up,' Asha said. 'It's not *my* fault that

you're arguing.'

'You've ruined everything,' Sal said, his voice rising to a crescendo. His hands had clenched involuntarily into fists. He gritted his teeth. 'Everything was fine. Everything was good.'

Even as he said it, he knew the words were a lie. Things had been *too* good, like a house of cards that quaked and shivered in the stillest of air. So precarious, he had hardly dared breathe for fear of disturbing it. It was almost a relief to have it all come crashing down around him.

Asha hissed out a breath. 'No, it wasn't, Sal. He needed to know.'

'He didn't.' Sal slammed his hand against the wall. 'He couldn't handle it. He *can't* handle it.'

'He loves you, Salem,' Asha snapped. 'You can't lie to people who love you.'

Sal shook his head. He shoved past her, feeling a vicious rush of satisfaction when she let out a soft exhale of pain. 'He doesn't,' he said. 'Not any more.'

Back in his room, he flicked through the pages of his sketchbook. It had changed. Pages and pages of drawings of skeletons and ghosts had gradually morphed into pages filled with intricately carved pumpkins and steaming coffee cups. There were pointy witches' hats, and sunsets over cornfields, and an entire page dedicated to a pair of big grey eyes.

The reason, Sal thought, that he hadn't been able to share the truth was that there was a part of him that *wanted* the house to be haunted. That wanted his dad's spirit to linger on. That craved the nights when he could smell his cigarette smoke, drifting up from the porch. Or hear him humming as he passed by outside Sal's door. It was the same part of him that half believed his mother was still there with them. The part that saw her in the night, midway between sleep and waking, standing in the doorway of his room. That still woke up every morning and took a minute to realize she had left. He was still clinging to the ghost of his old life. It was easier than accepting it was gone.

He slammed the book closed and lay down on the bed, unmoving. He awoke to the red light of sunset seeping through the curtains and kicked off his jeans before crawling under the covers. The next day was a Saturday, and he had nowhere to be and no one to see. He lifted the pillow over his head and decided that remaining in bed for the entire weekend was a perfectly reasonable plan.

For two days, he stayed in his room. He tried sketching, but his hands weren't doing what his head wanted them to. He spent more time erasing lines than he did drawing them. He tried watching films too, but kept getting to the end and realizing he hadn't paid any attention. Every so often, he got off the bed and looked out of the window, half expecting to see Pax walking up the drive. He emerged only for food, avoiding Asha as much as possible, and ignoring her if she made any attempt to speak to him. A permanent sinking sensation had settled in his chest, and he spent hours staring at the ceiling, waiting for it to lift.

On Monday morning Sal set off early to school for the first time in his memory, solely for the purpose of avoiding Dirk. It had rained overnight and the crisp autumn leaves that covered the driveway had turned into a sludgy brown soup that squelched beneath his shoes. The walk seemed longer alone.

When he reached the school, the eyes of other students lit up at his presence, taking a sick satisfaction in the drama. Sal kept his head down, but could still feel their burning gazes, hot on the exposed skin of his neck. In that moment, he hated every last one of them. They had broken into the darkest corners of his life and mined them for their own entertainment.

Dirk found him by the lockers. He shook his head at him and clucked his tongue in mocking disapproval. The gesture made Sal burn with irritation. He stuck his head in his locker, ignoring him as he rummaged through its contents.

'Hey,' Dirk said, catching sight of his face and resting a hand on his shoulder. 'Tough luck about your mum.'

Sal shrugged him off. 'I don't want to talk about it.'

'Yeah,' Dirk said breezily. 'I worked that out. What with you never having mentioned it. Brave of Asha to write the article, though, right?'

Every conversation Sal had with Dirk came back to Asha. He was beginning to wonder if she was the only reason they were friends. He ignored the question. There was nobody he wanted to talk about less.

'You're still pissed at me, aren't you?' Dirk said, unwrapping a stick of gum. 'I'm not going to apologize. You should have told her that you and Pax are together.'

Sal closed his locker with more force than was strictly necessary. The clang of metal caused heads to turn. 'We're not.'

'What?' Dirk looked startled.

'We're not,' Sal repeated. He stepped forward, blood pounding in his temples, and pressed a finger into Dirk's chest. More people were watching, hands paused on their locker combinations as they turned to gawp. 'And you know what?'

Dirk's dark skin flushed. He held up his hands in surrender, pulling a face that said he thought Sal was being incredibly unreasonable. Sal thought he might have a point, which served only to make him angrier.

'What?' Dirk asked.

'For once, just for *once*, it would be nice if you were on my side.'

'I *am*,' Dirk protested.

'No, you're not,' Sal said. 'You're on Asha's side. Which is *pathetic*, by the way. She doesn't even like you.'

He turned his back on him and strode away down the corridor, his vision blurred by anger. Behind him, someone broke the silence with a muffled laugh. He spotted Pax by the door to the library and the boy turned away and disappeared inside, avoiding his gaze. Elsie was following him, and she scrunched her nose up in confusion as Sal approached.

She reached out to grab his arm and he shook her off and kept walking, leaving the blurring sea of faces behind.

CHAPTER TWENTY-SEVEN

That evening, the doorbell rang. Sal flung himself at his bedroom window, expecting to see Pax on the porch below. It was Annie. She was wrapped in a beige coat and shivering in the wind. She looked very small in front of the towering doorway. Sal ducked away from the window and waited, unmoving, for her to leave. When he dared to glance back outside, she was at the end of the drive, struggling over the gate with difficulty, the ivy tangling around her legs.

The phone rang a couple of hours later, as Asha was getting in from work, and he slipped downstairs in time to see her pick it up.

'Who?' she asked, voice cautious. 'Oh! Pax's mum?'

She was in the living room, curled up on the sofa, with her back to him. She was nodding pointlessly as she listened, twirling the ties of her work apron around her fingers.

'We're fine, thank you. He's fine.'

She was silent for a long time, and then she apologized for something. She sounded like she meant it.

'He'll be OK.'

Sal turned away and went back upstairs, not bothering to lighten the thud of his footsteps.

He was half waiting for things to get worse. For another paper to pick up the story. For social services to turn up at the door. Asha hadn't yet turned eighteen, and even when she did, Sal wasn't sure if it would be enough to protect him too. He was also half waiting for things to get better. For someone to show up and offer them help. To tell them what to do. To tell them how to cope.

But nothing changed, and it occurred to Sal, slowly and then all at once, that nobody actually cared. Flocks of people weren't rushing to see if they were OK. The story wasn't being reposted online. Even at school, within a couple of days, people had stopped talking about it.

Mr Gulliver had dragged him into the office for a heart to heart, but when Sal had told him everything was fine, for the twentieth time, he decided to believe him and waved him back out of the door.

School became a constant struggle. Sal enjoyed Dirk's company more than he liked to let on, and school without him was hard work. Everyone liked Dirk, and people tolerated Sal simply because he was Dirk's friend. Their friendship had acted as a constant buffer, keeping the remnants of Sal's social life intact.

Sal hadn't spoken to Pax since they'd argued, and the only person at school still willing to talk to him was Elsie. Unfortunately she had also become Pax's best friend, and seemed to think spending too much time with Sal would amount to a betrayal. He was limited to awkward, muttered discussions with her in English class, and the occasional friendly wave in the corridors.

He started avoiding the common room. Wherever he went he felt as though a thousand eyes were upon him, marking him as a stranger, as an outcast. Walking into crowded spaces began to make his chest feel too tight, as though there wasn't enough air left over for him. He wondered if this was how Pax had felt during all the time he had spent on his own, and he hated himself for being one of the people who had turned his back on him.

He started smoking more. Not because he enjoyed it – mostly it just made him cough. But it was a good reason to sit outside alone and not have to confront the sixth-form common room.

Elsie found him outside one day and sat down next to him on the grassy slope that led to the woods. She must have put in some effort to find him. The slope was out of sight, over a grassy verge behind the playing fields on the very edge of the school grounds. The woods spread out below him, and the spire of the church marked the outskirts of the village beyond it. In summer, it was a popular place to sit but now it was cold, and Sal was alone.

'Hey, heartbreaker,' Elsie said, elbowing him in the ribs.

'Pax is devastated.'

Her tone was light, but Sal could hear the accusation in her words.

'I didn't break up with him,' he said. He hadn't, really. Things had just fallen apart.

'You lied to him. About your mum.'

Sal stubbed out his cigarette into the ground, grinding the stub down to soggy ash amid the grass. He glared out over the woods, watching a flock of birds emerge, screeching, from a distant thicket of trees. 'I'm pretty sure that's none of your business, Elsie.'

Elsie sighed and stood up, brushing down her skirt. 'You need to stop pushing people away.'

'I'm not,' Sal said. He didn't believe in running after people. Or in begging people to stay. If people wanted to stay, they did. 'They're leaving voluntarily.'

Elsie sat back down.

'I didn't mean I wanted *you* to stay,' Sal said. He was being petty and he knew it. But he was too proud to be glad of her company.

'Yeah, well.' She lay back, despite the chill of the ground, folding her arms behind her head and staring up at the bleak, cloudy sky. 'Tough shit.'

There was a companionable silence for about as long as Sal had ever known Elsie to be silent. She shuffled around on the grass, rolling on to her side to get a better look at him. She looked him up and down, obviously near bursting with the desire to speak.

'What?' Sal grumbled.

'Do you miss him?' she asked.

Sal didn't reply.

He hadn't seen much of Pax over the past few days. When he did see him, he looked miserable, and Sal hated that he found that kind of comforting. They sat at opposite ends of the room in art class and Sal got the impression that they kept missing each other's gaze. He would turn around to see Pax's head whipping in the other direction, or lower his own head whenever Pax was about to catch him looking.

Elsie and Pax had laid claim to the library, and though Elsie insisted that he could still join them, Sal couldn't think of anything he might find more awkward.

It seemed ridiculously contrary, but somehow falling out with Pax had led him to develop an even more suffocating crush on him. He couldn't look at him any more without his insides performing acrobatics. Or hear his voice without his heart skipping a beat. He felt as though his body had cruelly betrayed him.

'He'd forgive you,' Elsie said. 'If you let him.'

He squeezed his eyes closed and fisted his hands in the grass at his sides. Perhaps Elsie was right, he thought. But he didn't think he could live with the possibility that she might be wrong.

'Asha should never have written that article,' he said. To his horror he felt his eyes welling up. He squeezed them closed, forcing the tears back inside.

'Maybe she just needed to talk about it,' Elsie said. 'Do you think your mum will come back?'

'I don't know,' Sal said, frowning.

Elsie bit her lip. 'But is she OK?'

Sal remembered how much he liked Elsie. She was the first person who had asked him that. Who had acted like their mum was anything other than a monster, for leaving them. 'She doesn't really *do* OK.'

Elsie smiled at that. She raised an eyebrow. 'Does anyone?'

'No,' Sal said, huffing out a laugh. 'No, I guess not.'

Sal lay back in the grass next to her and watched the clouds above them drag by. He lit another cigarette and watched the smoke disappear into nothingness while the ash formed a crumbling tower reaching towards the sky and the paper burnt down to his fingers.

'I don't know if anyone really believed the house was haunted,' Elsie said, after several minutes of silence had passed.

Sal turned his head to frown at her in confusion. He had grown up believing the rumours that circled about his house. He had told his friends on the school playground and they had told their parents. And their parents had laughed it off until they heard it again from someone else, and then again, and again. It had become easier to believe than disbelieve. And then it was village lore. Number seventeen Yew Tree Lane was haunted.

'I think they just knew something wasn't right,' Elsie continued. 'And they didn't know how to handle it.'

'I think you'd like my sister,' Sal told her, when the bell rang and they were forced to stand up and stretch their cold-stiffened limbs.

'You should introduce us.'

Sal tried to remember the last time he had seen Asha with another girl her own age. Or with anyone her own age. Or with anyone at all.

'I can't,' he said, feeling a stab of guilt. 'We're not talking.'

Elsie rolled her eyes. 'Of course you're not. Does stubbornness run in the family?'

Sal smiled reluctantly. He thought it probably did. He had learnt his own from Asha's. He supposed their mother must have her fair share too. Or, by now, she would surely have come home.

The school bell continued to ring in the distance, in one long alarm-like peal. They walked back towards the school together, chilled to the bone, their clothes damp from the grass. As they approached the doors, Elsie linked her arm through his.

'Why are *you* still talking to me?' Sal asked. 'I lied to you too, y'know.'

'Yes,' Elsie said. 'But *I* always thought you were hiding something. Unlike Pax, I don't think you're the best thing since sliced bread.'

Sal laughed. 'Fair enough. What *do* you think?'

'I think you're no more or less fucked up than the rest of us.'

'Thanks,' Sal said. 'That actually kind of helps.'

Elsie grinned. 'Any time.'

CHAPTER TWENTY-EIGHT

Not talking to Asha was just plain hard work. The fragile ecosystem of their household relied on Sal and Asha talking to each other. They were, after all, the only two people in the house.

Sal didn't see her dressed up to go to the *Herald* again. When she left for work in the mornings, she was wearing her shop apron. She told him she had quit the internship, but it wasn't enough to make him want to speak to her again.

What little routine they'd had began to fall apart. Asha had been up to the attic and turned off their mum's radio. It felt too quiet without it. In the kitchen, Sal threw the abandoned coffee pot away, and scrubbed clean the mug that Mum had left on the countertop. He tucked it away in the back of one of the cupboards, where he wouldn't have to look at it. When Asha was in the house, Sal didn't leave his bedroom. They ate separately. Asha left him meals that he refused to eat, living on junk food instead.

They no longer spent evenings together in front of the fire. Asha stopped lighting it and the house felt cold and dank.

Sal felt as though he had developed a bruise some-where deep inside his chest. He felt sore inside, like an apple turned brown and tender under the skin. If he stayed still, the pain was more manageable, so that was exactly what he did. He didn't leave the house apart from for school.

After school on Wednesday, Sal collected a small pile of dew-damp letters that the postman had thrown over the gate and into the garden. There was an early birthday card for Asha. Sal recognized the writing on the envelope – neat, calligraphic swirls belonging to his grandma in Egypt. There was an assortment of junk mail too, and, beneath it all, a thick white envelope with Asha's full name printed on the front. He left the post in the kitchen, made himself a mug of coffee and four slices of hot, buttered toast, then headed back up the stairs.

Halfway up, he froze. He remembered the letter he had written on Dirk's laptop, and signed, stamped and posted to London. He took the stairs back down three at a time, sloshing coffee against the walls in his wake and sending a piece of toast flying over the banister.

Back in the kitchen, he grabbed the envelope, shoved it into his hoodie pocket and careered back up the stairs, slamming his bedroom door behind him. He dropped on to the bed, pulled out the letter, and tore open the envelope.

Dear Asha Rose Amani,
We are writing to inform you that, in light of your extenuating circumstances, we have accepted your request to begin your studies in January . . .

He read the contents twice, and once more for good measure, his heart thudding in his chest. He folded it carefully back up and slipped it back into the envelope.

Outside, the sun had set. It was a still night and the house felt very quiet. He could hear only the soft creaking of the yew tree outside his window and the buzz of his television left on standby.

Downstairs, the front door creaked open and slammed closed as Asha shouted a tired 'hello' up the stairs.

It had been a bad idea, Sal thought. Asha would be angry at him for interfering. She didn't even like leaving the house for work, never mind to go and live halfway across the country.

She probably wouldn't even have wanted to go. Not really. She had torn down all the old articles that papered the walls of her bedroom. Sal had found them lying, crumpled and curling, under broken eggshells in the kitchen bin.

He leant down and hid the letter under the loose floorboard in the middle of the room, ignoring the guilt that licked at the edges of his consciousness. If their mum had never left, Sal thought, Asha would already have been at university. But one night in September had changed everything, and he couldn't stop playing it, over and over, in his mind.

CHAPTER TWENTY-NINE

It had started out as a normal day. Asha had been busy working at the shop, and Sal had been busy lying on his back in his room, listening to The Smiths on repeat. It was late, when he finally headed downstairs. He found his mum in the kitchen, draining the dregs from the coffee pot into her mug, although it was close to nine at night. None of them had eaten, and Asha was rummaging through the fridge, trying to find something to cook. Sal could tell she was stressed by the tension in her shoulders.

'Your dad hates eating late,' their mum said, staring into her cup.

It was a habit she had held on to – referring to their dad in the present tense. Asha normally let it go, but this time the words set her immediately on edge. When she turned to face their mum, her eyes were dark and fiery.

'Hated,' she corrected. 'He's gone.'

'He's not gone.' Their mum's eyes filled instantly with tears. 'Not really. You just can't see the others in this house like I can.'

'I can see he's not here,' Asha said, coldly. She gestured at Sal. '*We're* still here, though. Remember us? We're your children, you're supposed to be looking after us, not the other way round.'

'I *am* looking after you.' Their mum pressed her hands to her eyes, forcing back the tears. She stood up, brushed herself down and steered Asha out of the way of the fridge. She inspected its contents: a few limp vegetables and a half-empty carton of orange juice. She sighed. 'I'm trying to.'

'Maybe we should just order pizza?' Sal suggested.

'We had pizza yesterday,' Asha said. 'I had it for lunch too.'

'Curry then,' their mum decided.

'I'm sick of takeaway food,' Asha said. 'Can't we just cook something?'

'If you think you can conjure something up with *that*,' their mum gestured at the contents of the fridge, 'then be my guest.'

'You said you'd go shopping today,' Asha said, accusingly.

'I know.' Their mum closed the fridge and opened the drawer where they kept their takeaway menus. 'I'll go tomorrow. I promise.'

'Don't bother,' Asha said. She leant back against the

kitchen table and folded her arms. 'I'll pick some stuff up at work. I'd hate to distract you from sitting around, imagining Dad's still here.'

Sal wished she would let it go.

'I'm not imagining it,' their mum said. 'I still hear his voice. So *clearly* sometimes.' She turned to Sal. 'You can hear him too, can't you, Sal?'

'No he can't!' Asha protested.

Sal said nothing, uncomfortable at being dragged into the argument. Asha and his mum had never got on well. And since Dad had died, Sal was always the one stuck in the middle, trying to bridge the gap between them. The hunger pains that had pulled him downstairs had been replaced with an unpleasant churning sensation in his stomach. He could feel Asha's anger flooding through the room when he didn't immediately take her side.

'You can,' his mum pressed, trying to catch Sal's eye. 'We've talked about it – in the middle of the night. Your dad's still here, Sal.'

'I don't know, Mum,' he said, avoiding her eye. 'Maybe.'

'He can't see or hear Dad,' Asha interrupted. 'Because, unlike you, he's moving on.' She jabbed a finger, hard, into Sal's chest. '*He's* getting on with his life. He's still living it.'

Their mum kneaded her fists against her closed eyes. Her voice, when it came, was uncharacteristically sharp. 'Why do you always have to make things difficult, Asha?'

Sal winced before Asha had even reacted, the words like a punch in the gut. Asha tossed her head back and half laughed, staring up at the ceiling. Then she stormed forwards and slammed her hands on the kitchen table.

'He's dead,' she shouted.

His mum was shaking with anger. She picked the coffee cup up off the table and threw it across the room. It smashed against the wall, less than a metre from where Sal was standing, forcing him to duck as shards of china flew, spinning, through the air.

The crash was followed by a heavy silence, broken only by Asha – breathing as if she had just run a marathon. Sal kicked at the broken china on the floor. It looked like broken bones against the red terracotta of the tiles. The anger left their mum's face at the sight of it. She knelt down, fingers trembling as she began collecting the shards.

'I wish you'd just leave,' Asha said, watching her. She wasn't shouting any more. Her voice was quiet. 'I can't stand living with you any more.'

'You don't mean that,' their mum said tightly.

'I do.' Asha folded her arms across her chest. 'We'd be better off without you. You make everything worse.'

Their mum glanced up at Sal, pleading silently for him to disagree with Asha. Sal met her eye. He opened his mouth to speak, but found he didn't know what to say. His mum dropped the pieces of china she was holding and stood up. She pushed past Asha, and then past Sal, and walked, slowly and purposefully, up the stairs.

They heard her bedroom door slam, and the sound of things being thrown around inside.

'I think you should go after her,' Sal told Asha. He had

been biting at the skin around his fingernails while he listened, and it was starting to bleed. 'Try and make up.'

Asha turned on him, with the same fury she had shown their mother just seconds before.

'Of course you do, Sal,' she spat at him, voice full of venom. 'Wouldn't that be nice and easy for you?'

'Screw you,' Sal said, anxiety turning to a sharp flare of anger. 'I'm on your side.' He moved round her into the lounge, and threw himself on the sofa, folding his arms across his face, and half listening to the noise of movement from above him.

Asha followed him in five minutes later, and poked him in the ribs.

'What?' he said, unmoving. He could hear the sounds of the bathroom cupboards being ransacked upstairs.

'I didn't mean it,' Asha said.

Sal lifted his arms and blinked at her. She was chewing her lips, a frown etched deep into her forehead.

'So tell her you're sorry,' he said.

'No,' Asha said. 'I meant what I said to her. I didn't mean what I said to you.'

They were interrupted by the sound of something heavy being dragged down the stairs. And when they emerged from the lounge together they were greeted by the sight of their mother, face pale and stained with tears, dragging her suitcase down behind her.

Sal watched his mum wrestle the zip closed on her bag, and pull her jacket out from the pile of coats that perpetually lived on the banisters.

'You're not actually going, are you?' Sal asked. 'Asha didn't mean it.'

Asha said nothing. Her arms were folded as she watched. If it weren't for how her jaw was twitching, Sal wouldn't have known she was upset.

Their mum pulled her shoes from the back of the hall cupboard, and laced them with trembling fingers. It was the first time Sal had seen her leave the house in weeks.

'Wait.' Sal was already reaching for his trainers. 'We can come with you. You just need a break. We can all go somewhere, right Asha?'

'No.' His mum shook her head, not meeting his eye. 'No, Sal, Asha was right. I need to get my head straight. Find some peace.'

'When are you coming back?' Sal asked, his voice breaking.

'I don't know,' their mum said. She opened the front door and hesitated, looking back at them one last time before stepping through it and slamming it closed behind her with a loud, echoing bang.

'She won't go,' Sal said.

From outside came the sound of the car's ignition roaring into life. Asha pulled the door back open in time for them to see it rolling away down the drive.

'Fine,' Asha said, watching their mum turn out of the gate and disappear from sight. 'That's just fine.'

She left Sal standing, flabbergasted, at the front door, and disappeared back into the lounge. There was the sound of something being kicked over. When Sal followed her, he found the coffee table on its side, and Asha lying face down on the sofa, screaming silently into a cushion.

At first, they had expected her to come back. They had left the driveway gate open for weeks, until one day Asha cracked, and pulled it back closed with such force that it fell off its hinges, and half sank into the ground. Ivy had crawled over it in the weeks that followed, tying it closed. It grew too quickly, as if the house was sealing them in, or stitching closed the wound their mum had left when she tore herself free of it.

CHAPTER THIRTY

It was the 19th of November, the day before Asha's eighteenth birthday, and autumn was giving way to winter. When Sal walked home that evening, there was a cold bite to the wind and the sky was a dank, dreary grey as endless clouds whipped by overhead. As he approached the house, he knew in the pit of his stomach that something was wrong.

Asha was sitting, ashen-faced, on the front steps, dressed only in leggings and a baggy T-shirt, despite the autumn chill. She had her phone clutched to her ear and looked like she was listening very carefully. At the sight of him, she got to her feet and walked barefoot down the gravel driveway.

Sal broke into a run, anxious to reach her.

'Yes, OK,' she said, voice strangely formal, as Sal rushed

into hearing distance. 'We'll be there.'

'It's Mum, isn't it?' Sal said, certain this explained the frozen expression on Asha's face. His heart lurched with relief at the realization that she had called them and wanted to see them. The bone-deep knowledge that everything, finally, was going to be OK. He reached for the phone, unable to stop himself grinning. 'Let me speak to her.'

Asha took a step backwards, and he lunged forward and grabbed the phone from her ear, just in time to hear the click of the receiver at the other end of the line.

'It wasn't her,' Asha said, voice so quiet it was nearly whipped away by the wind. 'It was the police.'

'What?' Sal frowned. 'What do you mean?'

'She's been taken to hospital,' Asha said, her voice cracking. 'She crashed the car.'

'Which hospital?' Sal heard himself asking. 'Where is she?'

'In town.' Asha's voice sounded like it was coming from very far away. 'I think she was coming back.'

Sal's head felt thick, and cloudy, and his eyes were blurred. There was a pounding in his ears, as though he had been suddenly submerged in hot bathwater.

'Is she—' He couldn't finish the sentence.

'They said it's serious,' Asha said. 'We need to go now.'

Sal made it to the front door before his legs collapsed beneath him and he sank down on to the frosty stone, as Asha looked on, helpless, at his side.

'We need to go,' she repeated, even as she sank on to

the step next to him.

Sal nodded. He was waiting for Asha to tell him how they were going to get there. When she said nothing else, he turned to look at her. It occurred to him, for the first time, that she still looked very young. She had lost weight in the last year, and looked too thin. Goosebumps had risen along the exposed skin of her arms. Her cheeks were colourless and her eyes were wide and unblinking. Her entire body was trembling.

She saw him looking, and he watched her pull herself back together, her eyes focusing as she stood. She winced when she was on her feet, and lifted a bare foot so she could brush off the gravel that had embedded itself in it, one hand gripping the pillar of the porch for support. 'I'll call a taxi.'

Sal shook his head. The nearest taxi company was based in town, twenty minutes away. He drew his phone out of his pocket, flicked through his contact list without thinking, and dialled.

'Hello?' said the voice at the other end of the line.

'Need the car,' Sal said. His words weren't coming out properly and he tried to clear his throat but just sounded like he was choking. 'Hospital. My mum. Thanks.'

Somewhere in the sky above them, the sun must have been setting. They could not see it, but its bleeding rays were seeping into the clouds, turning their grey plumes a murky shade of red.

CHAPTER THIRTY-ONE

irk arrived in a shriek of wheelspin five minutes later. He jumped out and pulled Sal into a rough hug before forcibly manhandling him into the passenger seat. He opened the back door for Asha and threw himself into the driver's seat. The engine coughed and spluttered three times before it finally cranked into life, and they skidded out of the driveway at terrifying speed.

'*Dirk*,' Asha said, leaning forward from the back seat. Now that they were moving, she seemed to have recovered some of her usual self-assurance.

'Yes?'

'It won't help if we end up in a crash too.'

Sal had never seen the village flash by so quickly. The lights were on in Pax's house and he pictured him quietly sipping tea with Annie in the kitchen and wondered how he had ever thought they could be together. They drove past the shadowy church and its crumbling gravestones, on past the farm and its rotting pumpkin patch, down the track that led over the rolling fields and finally, out and on to the main road.

It was beginning to rain, a soft, gentle smattering of drops that didn't seem to fit the gravity of the situation. As they approached the town, they were forced to slow down and became caught in a blockade of rush-hour traffic. It felt like winter had set in early on the cold, grey streets they drove down: each one colourless, lined with bare-branched trees and cold metal railings.

'I'm glad you called me,' Dirk said, while they waited for the fourth set of traffic lights to change. He was gripping the steering wheel tightly, even though they weren't moving. His knuckles had turned white.

Sal looked away. 'I didn't have a whole lotta options.'

He didn't want to admit how much Dirk's presence was helping. It felt good to see him again, even if it was under the worst of circumstances.

They didn't know where to go, so Dirk drove them to the doors of the A&E. The rain had turned to sleet, and Asha was still in her leggings and T-shirt. Dirk wriggled out of his coat as she got out of the car, and flung it out of the passenger door at her, before she could close it. She caught it and frowned, and Dirk reached over and pulled the passenger door closed before she could throw it back at him. He pulled off in search of a parking space, and Sal dragged Asha away through the doors.

When they entered the hospital, time became a blur. Asha bypassed reception and grabbed hold of a harried-looking nurse instead. The nurse heard the urgency in her voice and led them up a flight of stairs and down a maze of corridors to another desk. The woman behind it told them their mother had been wheeled through a set of doors through which they were not allowed to pass. She wouldn't tell them how she was.

'If you want to wait here,' she said, as if they had any other option, 'the doctor will come and speak to you when he can.'

They sat on red plastic chairs in the bright white chasm of the corridor and listened to the tread of squeaky foot-steps on polished vinyl floors. The hospital smelt of rubber, and of cheap liquid hand soap. Sal burrowed his nose and mouth in the sleeves of his hoodie and inhaled deeply. There was still the faint scent of sage.

He missed Pax.

He missed the curls of his hair.

He missed his stupid clothes.

He missed his knitted hat with the reindeer antlers.

He missed his big grey eyes and the way he blinked at Sal like he was looking directly into sunlight.

He missed the smell of incense that lingered on his skin.

He missed Annie's apple pie and custard, and the way she shouted up the stairs at them if they ever dared to close the bedroom door.

He missed the press of Pax's lips and the cold of his

222

hands and the warmth of his arms.

Nobody made him feel safe the way that Pax did. Even when the boy was waving a stem of burning sage around and at serious risk of setting his house on fire.

Dirk didn't appear, but Sal remembered the bear hug he had dragged him into back on the driveway and figured this wasn't for lack of trying. They sat alone. The clock ticked out the endless seconds. Asha got up to interrogate the nurse, got nowhere and sat back down.

Sal couldn't cry. He was aware it was the thing to do, but the tears just weren't coming. He figured Asha was having trouble too, because she kept staring into the fluorescent lights above them and blinking rapidly and then looking back down at the floor, dry-eyed and confused.

They were speaking again. They were speaking by unspoken agreement and had been ever since Asha had answered the call from the police. Since Sal had turned the corner and seen her, broken but waiting for him on the porch of their house.

But Asha, for once, didn't have much to say. It was cold in the corridor, and she had pulled on Dirk's coat. The sleeves were too long for her, and she was fisting her hands in them, tugging at the fabric. She kept muttering under her breath. The same thing over and over again. *It's my fault. It's my fault. It's my fault.*

The sound was making Sal feel faintly nauseous. She turned to look at him. Her hand sought his and gripped it. Cold and clammy against his own.

'It's my fault,' she said in a raspy voice, with such

certainty that it took Sal a second to correct her.

He remembered Asha's face, contorted with anger, on the night of the argument. The night she had finally cracked, exhausted from years of looking after her own mother. Of looking after Sal too. Ever since their father had died, Asha had been picking up the slack. She had often bought the food, and paid the bills when Mum forgot, and cleaned the house – because Mum didn't see the mess – and tried to get Sal to do his homework. Mum had usually managed the basics, but she hadn't done much else.

'Don't be stupid,' Sal said. 'How could a car crash be your fault?'

A doctor emerged through the swinging grey doors at the end of the corridor. He looked around with a blank expression. The nurse had to stand up, tap his shoulder and point him towards them. It took him a second to mask his expression of surprise. With their golden-brown skin and dark hair, they bore little resemblance to their mother. They stood up as he approached, and he held out his hand as if they were at a business conference, not a hospital.

Asha stepped forward, back in charge now that she was no longer visibly shaking. Under the bright lights of the hospital, she looked older. There were lines prematurely etched into her forehead and dark circles under her eyes.

She gave the doctor's hand a perfunctory shake and dropped it as if the contact was hurting her. He tried to usher them through to a private room, but she stood her ground. Sal was grateful. He was still holding the back of his chair. He thought his legs might give way if he moved.

'*Well?*' Asha asked. 'Is she alive?'

CHAPTER THIRTY-TWO

Sal could remember, with blinding clarity, the first time he had seen his mother cry. The first time his brain had made the electric-shock connection between her open mouth and the unearthly sounds that had drawn him out of bed that night.

He had come downstairs in time to see the police officers leaving, catching the way their eyes fell on him, full of pity before they stepped out of the door. His mum was knelt on the floor in the living room, doubled over as if crippled by pain. Her whole body wracked with the cries being drawn out of her. Her fists were clenched against the coffee table and her eyes squeezed so tightly closed that it seemed impossible that so many tears could escape them.

There was no sign of any injury. No wound to be

treated. But her pain was tangible. It filled the space around her and stole the oxygen from the room. Sal remembered wanting to help her but being too scared to get any closer.

He remembered clasping his hands to his ears and standing frozen in the doorway. It was Asha who pulled him away, who told him what the police had said. He remembered the way her voice held so steady and strong as she told him, over her own mother's cries, that their dad was dead.

The weeks that followed were, for Sal, a blur of closed doors and whispered conversations. He had been allowed to stay off school, but Sal's mum barely noticed when Asha and Sal were there, and when she did, she hugged them too hard and cried into their hair.

So, after two days, he had packed his own lunch and gone back, unable to bear being in the house. The other kids hadn't known how to talk to him at school. Sal let them keep their distance. All apart from Dirk, who found him sat alone one day in the playground and then wouldn't leave his side.

Their dad's family in Egypt flew in for the funeral. Their grandmother on their dad's side was too weak to travel, and their grandfather was cold and reserved. He shook their hands when they met him, but hardly spoke to their mother. He had never approved of her, she told them afterwards. Their aunts and uncles were kind – gave Sal and Asha hugs and gifts, and promised they could call them any time. But there were so many of them,

227

and their visit was so brief that Sal only just had a chance to put names to faces, before they were all on the plane back home – leaving Sal and Asha to face their haunting alone.

CHAPTER THIRTY-THREE

'She's alive,' the doctor said.

He managed to usher them through into a private room, where he rattled through a list of injuries so long that Sal could only just keep track of them all.

'. . . three broken ribs,' he finished. 'And a collapsed lung.'

He paused for breath and looked up at them. Sal thought he must have spotted the alarm on their faces, because he softened his tone, and asked if they wanted him to run through anything again.

'No,' Asha said, voice impatient. 'We're following. But is she going to be OK?'

'She's going to be fine,' he told them, finally smiling. 'The emergency surgery was very successful. But she'll need ongoing treatment, and the healing process will take a long time. She'll need to stay in the hospital for several weeks.'

'Can we see her?' Asha asked. 'Is she awake?'

'Not yet,' the doctor said. 'I'd advise you to go home and get some sleep. She might not wake up for a few hours.'

Asha's mouth was set in a determined line. 'We'll wait.'

The small room felt claustrophobic, the atmosphere stifling, and Sal let out a sigh of relief when they emerged back out on to the corridor.

He turned to Asha, raising an eyebrow. 'Now what?'

She looked back at him and opened her mouth to speak, but closed it again. Then she burst into tears and sank, in a crumpled heap, on to the scuffed linoleum floor. Sal didn't know if they were tears of relief or fear. He took her down to the cafeteria where she cried into a coffee cup and then all over the cinnamon bun he bought for her, until he told her she was ruining it and she half hiccupped, half laughed.

She reached over the table and grabbed his hand. 'I told myself I'd never let you see me cry.'

Sal squeezed her hand gently. It was almost a relief to see Asha cry. Somehow, it made the whole situation feel more normal. His own tears still weren't anywhere to be found.

'At least I know you're human now,' he said.

She wiped her eyes with the back of her free hand and made an attempt at a smile. 'How dare you, I'm invincible.'

'Well, yeah,' Sal agreed. 'You're that too.'

For some reason that set her off all over again, and Sal's

hand turned numb from how hard she was gripping it. They were surrounded by tables full of sad-looking people eating sad-looking food. Someone had painted the walls a sickly shade of yellow which Sal supposed was intended to look cheerful. The coffee was weak and watery, even without the addition of Asha's tears.

They sat there for half an hour while Asha licked at the cream-cheese frosting on top of her cinnamon bun, and Sal frowned down at his own hands.

When he finally thought to check his phone, he'd had three missed calls and a text from Dirk.

Dirk: They won't let me in. Fam only. Told them ur my bro but dont believe me. She gonna b ok?

Sal huffed out half a laugh and texted back.

Sal: She's ok. You should go home

He sat and thought for a second, and then shot off one more.

Sal: Thanks

'I'm glad you're talking to me again,' Asha said softly, once her tears had eased. She had licked all of the frosting off her cinnamon bun and was rolling tiny pieces into balls between her fingers.

'Only 'cause you're crying,' Sal lied, sticking his tongue out. 'I'd be a monster if I didn't.'

She reached over and punched him on the arm and he smiled reluctantly. *He* was glad they were talking again too. Not having Asha in his life had made him more miserable than he had thought possible.

'You *are* a monster,' Asha teased. 'But I missed you. And I'm really, *really* sorry. I should have asked you before I gave them that story. It should have been a joint decision.'

'OK,' Sal said. He shrugged and gazed out over the cafeteria. A family was arguing a few tables away. Two children squabbling and their mother trying to prise them apart. The sound of crying echoed through the cavernous room.

'Is that an *OK, I accept your apology*?' Asha asked. 'Or an *OK, I will tolerate you but still hate you*?'

'It's just an OK,' Sal said. 'And I'm sorry too.'

Asha blinked at him. 'What for?'

'I should have been more supportive,' Sal said. 'When you got the internship. I was being selfish.'

'You were right. It was the wrong thing to do.'

'But you were just trying to *do* something with your life,' Sal said.

'But what if she saw the article?' Asha asked, her face crumpling again. 'What if that's why she came back?'

It dawned on Sal that this had been what Asha meant when she said the accident had been her fault.

'I didn't write it because I was angry at her,' she continued, choking the words out. 'It was because I wanted to tell the truth. Really. But if she was driving, while she was upset . . . If she was distracted . . .'

'That's not what happened,' Sal said. 'You're overthinking it. She probably hasn't read the article. I bet no one even saw it outside of Holden.'

Asha dragged the heels of her hands across her eyes.

Sal moved around the table to sit next to her, slung an arm around her shoulders and squeezed. 'It's not your fault.'

When they went back upstairs, they moved out of the corridor and into a proper waiting room, a little further from where their mother lay unconscious. Everything was a very bright white. The floor had recently been mopped and was slick underfoot. The chairs looked as if they had been designed to inflict as much discomfort as possible. A vending machine hummed in the corner, a glowing beacon of light.

They sat there for an hour, before Asha disappeared to make a phone call. Sal could see her pacing up and down through the glass-panelled wall of the waiting room, frowning as she spoke. She glanced over at Sal and smiled when she saw him watching.

Sal pulled a sympathetic face and looked away towards the window. Night had fallen and he could see nothing but inky blackness and the shadowy form of his own reflection staring back at him. The hands of the waiting room clock were pointing to midnight. Across the waiting room a small child sat alone, fast asleep in his chair.

CHAPTER THIRTY-FOUR

Sal jerked awake in the waiting room. He had nodded off in the unforgiving vinyl chair and his neck was screaming in protest. The fluorescent light overhead was flickering on and off and Asha was sitting next to him, staring straight ahead. He checked his watch. It was past midnight.

'Happy birthday,' Sal said, his voice rasping.

'Oh yeah.' Asha checked her own watch. 'I forgot.'

Sal stretched out his cramped legs and yawned. 'What have I missed?'

'Two different people fighting the vending machine,' Asha said. 'Other than that, not much.'

Sal stretched, yawned and rumpled a hand through his hair. 'Could they make this place any more uncomfortable?'

'We should raid a store cupboard,' Asha said. 'I bet there

are spare pillows. And blankets. And maybe even some of those little pots of jelly. The ones with the fruit in.'

Sal's stomach grumbled, and he realized he hadn't eaten since lunchtime. He got up to go to the vending machine. 'Wish me luck.'

He was engaged in a half-hearted wrestling match over a bag of Maltesers when the door to the waiting room swung open. He turned around on instinct, hoping to see the doctor bringing them news.

Pax and Annie stood in the doorway.

They were both dressed partially in pyjamas. Annie was wearing a pair of tartan slippers and Pax was wearing a pair of pyjama trousers patterned with pumpkins beneath his long fur coat. His hair resembled a wild bird's nest, and he was carrying a very large bunch of flowers in clashing shades of orange and pink.

'Salem,' he called out, waving, as if Sal had a hope in hell of *not* noticing him. Everyone in the waiting room was staring at him.

'Hi,' Sal said, for lack of anything better to say. He became aware his heart had stopped then, because it kicked back in, beating double time.

Annie and Pax wound their way towards him through the rows of plastic seats. Annie reached him first and pulled him into a crushing hug. She was warm and smelt of talcum powder and camomile tea. Sal let her hold him until he thought he might be about to pass out from lack of oxygen, then wriggled free.

'I'm sorry, Salem,' she said. 'I should have asked,

about your mum. I should have known something wasn't right.'

Sal shook his head, the words not registering. He was watching Pax, who was gazing back at him from behind his giant bouquet of flowers, chewing his lip and looking as if the world might be ending. Annie glanced between them and pushed Pax towards him, before setting off towards Asha.

'I chose the flowers,' Pax said, gesturing needlessly at the violently coloured blooms. He sounded nervous, which Sal wasn't used to.

'Yeah,' Sal said. 'I can tell.'

At the other side of the room, Annie had pulled Asha into a hug too and Asha sent Sal a look of startled alarm over the woman's shoulder.

Help, she mouthed.

'I'm really sorry,' Pax said. He sounded a bit like his heart was breaking.

Sal cleared his throat. His voice was gravelly from lack of sleep. 'Me too. I wasn't thinking straight. I should have told you she'd left us.'

'No,' Pax said. 'Well . . . *yes*, actually, that would have been nice. But I should have realized. I just got caught up in trying to help. I liked thinking I was helping you.'

'You were,' Sal protested. 'You *were* helping. Just . . . not in the way you thought you were.'

It was true. Sal didn't think he'd ever been happier than when Pax had invaded his house (and his life) with his crystals, and his bunches of sage and his wreaths of

236

lavender. But Pax was looking at him as if he didn't, for one second, believe him. Sal hated it. Pax believed in everything.

Sal kicked his trainer against the shiny hospital floor and the rubber squealed against it. 'I missed you.'

Pax's expression cleared, as if somehow Sal had made everything very simple. He leant in and kissed him square on the mouth. 'I missed you too.'

Sal squeaked in surprise and took a hasty step back, hitting the vending machine as he glanced nervously around the waiting room.

A nurse was frowning at them from behind the desk in the corner. At the other side of the room, Annie had produced a book from her bag, and looked incredibly interested in it considering she was holding it upside down. Asha, meanwhile, was watching them. She was smiling properly for the first time since he had found her curled up in a heap on the front step.

Sal glared at her until she looked away, and then pulled Pax in, wrapping his arms around his waist. Pax's sleep-heavy eyes drifted closed, one hand lifting to land on Sal's jaw. His mouth was warm against Sal's and he stepped closer still, half crushing the flowers between their chests. From behind them there came the soft thunking sound of the bag of Maltesers falling, forgotten, from the machine.

'It's supposed to be family only in here,' Sal said.

They had settled in chairs across the room from Asha

and Annie. Pax was leaning into him, his head a warm and comforting weight against Sal's shoulder. The curls of his hair were tickling Sal's throat, and he could smell the warm, peachy scent of his shampoo.

'Oh,' Pax said. 'Yes. We told them I was your cousin.'

Sal supposed that explained why the nurse had frowned at them when they started kissing.

'How did you know what happened?' Sal asked.

'Asha called us,' Pax said. 'Didn't you know?'

Sal remembered her pacing up and down in the corridor, shooting him nervous looks as she spoke into the phone.

'I was asleep,' Pax said. 'But we came straight away.'

'That explains the pyjamas,' Sal said, looking down at his pumpkin-printed trousers.

Pax looked at him quizzically.

Sal sighed. 'They're just your regular clothes, aren't they?'

'Yes,' Pax said. He looked down at them and frowned in evident confusion. 'I got dressed. Why?'

Sal didn't answer. Across the room one of the nurses had approached Asha and was speaking to her in hushed tones. Asha stood and gave Sal a nervous thumbs up.

'Break it up, lovebirds,' she called across the room. 'It's time to go in.'

Pax stood up alongside Sal, who had to gently push him back down into his seat.

'Pax?' he said.

'Yes?'

'This is *not* how I want you to meet my mother.'

★

She looked very small, laid out in the hospital bed, and very fragile. There was a gauze bandage on her head and her right leg was in a brace. Her skin was nearly the same shade of white as the bed sheets. She was surrounded by an endless sprawling network of plastic tubes and a heart monitor beeped rhythmically at the side of the bed. Her eyes were closed.

'She's still half asleep,' the nurse said, identifying Asha as the adult and addressing her alone. 'But quite stable. We'll move her out of intensive care in the morning.'

Asha was too busy fussing over their mother to respond. She leant over her and pushed sweaty tendrils of hair back off her face, then kissed her on the forehead. She sank down into a chair at her side, exhaustion written into every flickering expression of her face.

'Where did you go?' she asked softly, taking hold of her hand.

Sal hovered behind her. He didn't know what to say to his mother at the best of times, never mind the worst.

She opened her eyes, staring straight up, unable to turn her head, and Sal saw a flicker of panic cross Asha's face, before she leant in to meet her gaze.

'Asha.' Their mum's voice was weak, and as she spoke, tears started falling down her cheeks. 'I'm sorry, Asha.'

'You don't need to be sorry,' Asha said, visibly relaxing. 'You just need to get better.'

Sal leant in too, feeling awkward. This wasn't how he

had expected to see her again, after two months apart. 'Hey, Mum.'

She lifted her free hand to take his. 'I'm sorry,' she said again, sleepily. 'I was coming home.'

CHAPTER THIRTY-FIVE

It was nearly two a.m. when Sal finally left the hospital with Annie and Pax. He had tried to persuade Asha to leave with them, but she wouldn't come, determined to stay by their mother's side.

He felt guilty for abandoning her, for escaping to the tranquillity of Pax's house. But it was a relief when Annie's car finally crunched up Yew Tree Lane, and the lights of the cottage came into view. Sal wondered how so much had happened in such a short space of time, and how the past evening had felt like the longest of his life. The time had dragged out, like a piece of elastic, stretched to breaking point before finally snapping back into just a short few hours of his past.

They sat in the tiny little living room just off the kitchen, drinking hot chocolate so rich that Sal could barely manage a sip. Pax downed his own in two mouth-fuls, sitting next to Sal on the sofa, their legs pressing together. In spite of everything, Sal started to feel sleepy on the floral-printed sofa, the carpet so thick his feet were sinking into it. Embers were glowing in the large stone fireplace and the room was warm and comforting.

Pax's mother said she thought they should try to get some sleep. She set up a bed for Sal on the sofa, digging out a set of old bed sheets covered with unicorns from the linen closet and bringing him a duvet and a tasselled cush-ion for a pillow, which smelt strongly of Pax. The boy looked reluctantly back over his shoulder as his mother ushered him away and up the stairs.

Inexplicitly, but very obviously, banned from Pax's room, Sal lay tossing and turning for hours, until the other boy arrived in the living room, barefoot and tousle-haired. He paused in the doorway, a soft silhouette against the grey dawn light streaming in through the windows behind him.

'I couldn't sleep,' he whispered.

'Me neither,' Sal murmured.

He tossed back the covers in silent invitation and Pax slunk in beside him, curling up against him. He was warm for once and Sal pulled him close and buried his face in his neck, breathing him in. He was so slender that Sal could count the notches of his spine as he ran his hand down his back. Everything felt, somehow, calmer.

'You're not OK,' Pax said.

Sal blinked at him through the gloom. 'Eh?'

'Well, I was going to ask,' Pax said, stealing more than his fair share of the duvet. 'But I realized I already knew the answer, so I just led with that instead.'

Sal tugged half the duvet back. 'That's not how conversation works, Pax.'

'Well,' Pax said, sniffing as the duvet was pulled out of his hands and wriggling in closer instead. '*Are* you OK?'

Sal rolled on to his back and stared at the ceiling. Pax's hand found his under the covers, where he tangled their fingers together.

'Are you scared?' he asked.

'No,' Sal lied. He lifted his head to meet Pax's eye. 'I don't get scared.'

Pax smiled in disbelief. 'Not of anything?'

'Not of anything,' Sal said. 'Apart from you. You're kind of terrifying.'

He let Pax laugh at him, drank in the sight until he started smiling too. Then they were both laughing, tears leaking from Sal's eyes. Then there were only tears and Pax was kissing them away, one by one, as they rolled down Sal's cheeks.

When there were no more tears to kiss away, Pax's lips met his. Kissing Pax was the best type of medicine because it made Sal's mind feel blissfully empty. All he had to think about was the press of his lips, made salty from tears, the drag of his hands and the occasional bump of his nose.

'Sorry,' Pax said eventually, when they had to stop and breathe. 'Don't you want to go to sleep?'

He sounded sheepish and made an attempt to wriggle

away from him, although the sofa left him no real space to move.

'No,' Sal said.

'Oh, OK.' Pax moved back in. 'Me neither.'

Sal was woken a few hours later by Pax's mother tapping on the living room door. When she opened it, her eyes narrowed at the sight of them curled up together. Pax had rolled over in his sleep and Sal was wrapped around his back, one arm slung over his waist. Under Annie's disapproving gaze, he awkwardly withdrew his arm and the boy made an annoyed grumbling noise in his sleep.

Annie pursed her lips, but they twitched as if she was suppressing a smile. Sal opened his mouth to speak and she shook her head. She was carrying a steaming cup of black coffee which she set down on the coffee table. When she left the room, she pulled the door gently closed behind her.

CHAPTER THIRTY-SIX

Annie and Pax dropped Sal off at the hospital a little after nine in the morning, but he refused their offer to come in with him. Pax was already halfway out of the car, and he began arguing but stopped abruptly when Annie glared at him. Sal squeezed his hand on the way out of the car by way of apology. He had begun the slow process of opening up to Pax, but he still wasn't quite ready to let him all the way in.

He went to the waiting room, but Asha was nowhere to be found. Then he went through to the ward where his mother had been, but the nurse said they had moved her out of intensive care and into a private room on another ward. Asha wasn't anywhere on the new ward either. When Sal poked his head into his mother's room, she was alone and sleeping. There was a little more colour in her cheeks, and she was no longer surrounded by quite so many wires and screens.

Eventually, he went down to the cafeteria, where he found Asha sprawled out, fast asleep in the corner. Her head had slumped forward on to the table and her mouth was open. There was a cold cup of coffee still clutched in her hand. Beneath her half-closed eyelids, her eyes were flickering as if she was dreaming.

Sal left her asleep and went to get her a replacement coffee and another cinnamon bun. She awoke when he set them on the table next to her and sat up with a start.

'Bollocks,' she said, loudly enough for the lady at the table nearest to them to look up and glare. Asha looked wildly around, disorientated. 'I was just gonna rest my head for a minute.'

Sal grinned. 'You need to sleep, Ash.'

'Have you been to see Mum?' Asha asked him.

'Yeah, she's sleeping too. They moved her out of intensive care, though.'

'I *know*,' Asha said, looking hurt. 'I stayed awake until then.'

Their mother was awake properly when they went back upstairs to visit her. Sunlight was starting to seep in through the windows of the room – lighting up the scuffed walls and peeling paint. Sal thought she looked anxious. He was nervous too – heart thumping in his chest. After everything that had happened, he wasn't sure how she would react to seeing him again.

He hadn't defended her, when she and Asha had argued. She'd looked to him for support and he'd stayed silent. He wasn't sure if she'd forgive him – he wasn't even sure he could forgive himself.

Asha held back, let him sit down on the only chair by the bed and muttered a vague excuse about getting more coffee, before retreating back out of the room, leaving them alone together. Sal glared at her retreating back. When he turned back to his mum, she was watching him. Sal had been so desperate to have her back that he hadn't fully thought through the consequences. It occurred to him that they probably wouldn't be able to have a normal conversation for a very long time. So he did what he did best, and stayed quiet.

'How are you, Sal?' his mum asked. She reached out and attempted to flatten his hair for him, and visibly winced when he shrugged her off.

'Sorry,' he said. There was something between them now that made any casual interaction seem somehow foreign, or fake. 'I'm OK.'

'I wish I hadn't left you,' his mother said. 'But I needed some time to sort out my head. It wasn't helping any of us, me being at home. Asha was right.'

'Yeah,' Sal agreed, not meeting her eye. 'She usually is.'

'Sal,' she said. She grabbed his hand. 'I'm sorry.' Her eyes were bright with tears and her jaw clenched with the effort of stopping them from falling. 'I really am. I've not been there for you since Dad died – not like I should have been.'

He nodded. This time, he let her hand rest in his. 'Where did you go?'

'I just kept driving,' she said. 'I couldn't stop. I moved to a new place each day. Slept in the car sometimes. I wasn't thinking straight.'

'You've just been driving around for two months?' Sal asked, doubtfully.

'Not the whole time,' she said. 'I looked up an old friend who lives in Scotland. In the middle of nowhere. I stayed with her for a while. Started working on my paintings again.'

'Did she know about us?' Sal asked. 'Me and Asha.'

His mum opened her mouth to reply, but hesitated, biting back the words before they left her tongue.

'You were pretending we didn't exist,' Sal said. The realization hit him like a punch in the gut. 'Do you wish we didn't?'

'No.' She gripped his hand tighter. 'God, no. Of course I don't, Sal. I need you. That's why I came back.'

'Yeah, well,' Sal said, turning his face away. 'We needed you too.'

'I'm sorry.' She let go of his hand and reached out to lift his chin, meeting his eye. 'I wish I could explain.'

Sal looked back at her. 'Try.'

'For the first time since your dad died, I felt . . .' She trailed off, staring down at her braced leg. 'I felt like I wasn't haunted,' she finished, eventually. 'It was a different place. A place that wasn't full of memories. Of ghosts. Do you understand?'

Sal wasn't sure he did. He watched the lines flickering on the monitor by the side of the bed.

'Were you all right?' she asked. 'While I was gone?'

Sal gave it some thought. 'Yeah,' he said. 'Yeah, I was.'

'And Asha?'

'Asha's always all right.'

Mum swallowed, as if her throat was dry. 'I wanted to be home for her birthday, you know. That's why I was rushing. I just wanted to be back in time.'

'Well,' Sal said. 'You made it.'

She smiled ruefully. 'This isn't exactly how I planned it would go.'

Sal helped himself to an unopened pot of jelly from the bedside table, and tore off the lid, suddenly ravenous.

His mum was watching him. 'I want to make things right again, Sal,' she said. 'With both of you.'

Asha arrived back as Sal was finishing the jelly, and gave him a disapproving look. She was carrying a tray of poly-styrene coffee cups, which she set down on the bedside table.

'How are you feeling?' she asked their mum. She nudged Sal out of the chair, and sat down on it herself, leaving him to hover awkwardly by the window. 'Do you need more pain relief?'

Their mum shook her head. She was twisting the fabric of the bed sheet around the fingers of her right hand. 'The doctors said I might need more surgery.' She nodded at the brace on her leg.

'They told us it might be a few weeks before you're

able to come home,' Asha agreed, brusquely.

'Is that what you want?' their mum asked. 'For me to come home?'

There was a moment of very tense silence. When Sal looked at Asha, he thought she might be about to implode.

'You're our *mother*,' she said. 'It's not supposed to be optional.'

Their mum opened her mouth, as if she was about to argue, and then thought better of it. 'You're right,' she agreed. 'I just . . .' She swallowed. 'I wasn't sure if you'd want me back. I know I rely on you too much, Asha. What you said to me that night, it was hard to hear but it was true.'

'It's your home,' Sal said. 'You belong there.'

'Exactly,' Asha agreed. 'But you need to face that Dad's really gone. We can't all keep tiptoeing around that fact.'

'I know he's gone,' their mum said. 'I do. I just couldn't let go. His memory is everywhere, in that house. But I'm ready to try and move on.'

'Then you'll come home,' Asha said decisively. She sipped at her coffee, slurping noisily in the quiet room. 'As soon as you're well enough. We'll make it work. We can move on together.'

Their mum started crying again, silent tears that Sal thought might be more from relief than from pain. She closed her eyes but the tears kept falling from behind her eyelids. Asha and Sal stayed with her while she cried, on either side of the bed, holding her hands.

They were there for what seemed like hours, until the tears stopped and her breathing deepened and she fell back into sleep. Asha reached out to smooth down her hair.

'Sorry about your birthday,' Sal said, once they were outside the hospital. They were stood in the rain-soaked car park, waiting for Annie and Pax to pick them up. 'It kind of sucked.'

'Never mind,' Asha said. Her clothes were crumpled from spending all night in the hospital, and she smelt strongly of coffee. She was still wearing Dirk's jacket, and had it pulled tightly around her to stave off the cold. 'I don't like birthdays anyway. They remind me I haven't done anything with my life.'

'You're *eighteen*,' Sal said.

'Exactly,' Asha said. 'S.E. Hinton had written *The Outsiders* by my age.'

'Yeah,' Sal said. 'I don't know who that is.'

Asha rolled her eyes and changed the subject. 'Are you happy?' she asked. 'That mum's coming home?'

'Yeah,' Sal said. 'I mean . . . I think I am.'

He squinted out through the drizzle. At the far end of the car park, he could see Annie's car pulling in off the road. He raised a hand and waved.

'I'm glad you and Pax made up,' Asha said.

'Yeah,' Sal said. He folded his arms across his chest and frowned, embarrassed that she had seen them kiss. 'Me too.'

'You did good,' Asha said, smiling. For the first time since Sal and Pax had met, she looked genuinely thrilled about the relationship. 'He's so . . . *weird*. I love it.'

Sal grinned, pleased to finally have her approval.

'I always thought I'd go for someone normal,' he said.

'Nah,' Asha said. 'You're too fucked up for that, bro.'

'Thanks, though,' Sal said, ignoring the jibe. 'For calling him. I wouldn't have done it.' His throat felt suddenly tight. 'I couldn't do it.'

Asha smiled at him. She reached out and ruffled his hair. 'I know.'

CHAPTER THIRTY-SEVEN

Sal had carried the secret of his mother's absence for so long that, without it, he felt disorientated. Like there was a great, gaping space inside him. He felt very light, almost hollow, sick with relief that she had returned, and regret that it had happened the way it had. And there was guilt too. As much as he wanted her home, a part of him couldn't forgive her for what she had done.

In preparation for her arrival, Asha had embarked on a massive cleaning spree, waging war on every dark, dusty corner of the house. She had cleaned the windows, and the house was bright inside for the first time in years. She had bought scented candles to conceal the smell of damp and lined them up on the mantlepiece. She had also opened the door to their mum's room for the first time since she'd left. Sal poked his head inside on his way past.

The room looked like a tornado had passed through it. Their mum had packed in a hurry, and all the drawers of the dresser had been left open, the clothes inside half spilling out on to the floor. The air in the room was musty and stale. There was a cup of tea growing thick, furry mould on the bedside table. The door to the adjoining bathroom was open. Inside, the shelves above the sink had been swept clean, and the remains of a broken glass bottle covered the floor. Asha was nowhere to be seen.

Sal found her downstairs, bundling their mum's bed sheets into the washing machine.

'We shouldn't have to do this,' she said, when she caught sight of him.

Asha hated doing laundry. But Sal was pretty sure that wasn't entirely the problem here. He recognized the bitterness in her voice. It was the same bitterness that had overflowed the night of their argument – the same bitterness that had driven their mum out of the door.

He frowned and picked up a stray pillowcase, throwing it into the drum just in time to avoid getting his hand trapped in the door when Asha slammed it closed. Their mum would be coming home on crutches. She wasn't going to be able to clean.

'She just needs some help.'

Asha was very carefully not looking at him as she turned the dial on the machine. 'She needs too much help.'

Sal watched her set the washing machine and give it the customary kick it always needed to get started. His mum wouldn't even know to do that, he realized. 'You're not going to forgive her, are you? I thought you said we were going to move on together?'

'I'm trying,' Asha said, wearily. 'I want to forgive her. It's just . . . she's going to have to build up trust again. And I just don't like her very much right now.'

'You don't like anyone,' Sal pointed out.

Asha narrowed her eyes at him. 'I like *you*,' she said. 'Most of the time.'

'I always thought I annoyed you,' Sal said.

'You do,' Asha said, with a grin. 'And you know what the worst part of all this is?'

'What?'

'I won't be in charge of you any more.'

'You're not in charge of me *now*,' Sal said.

Asha just smirked. 'Sure I'm not.'

Sal went back upstairs with Asha to help her finish the tidying. It was cold with the windows open, but the musty smell was starting to shift. He bundled the abandoned clothes back into the dresser, while Asha swept the broken glass from the floor in the bathroom. Sal had just thrown the last crumpled T-shirt back inside the dresser and was about to push the bottom drawer closed when something at the back of it caught his eye.

It was a thick stack of papers. On the top were drawings, crusted with glue and glitter and greasy wax crayon scribbles. Sal half remembered bringing them home from school, one by one, and handing them to his mother. Asha emerged from the bathroom as he was rifling through them, and picked up a drawing of a girl with long, dark braids and a boy with very messy hair, holding swords in the air as ghosts circled above them in a frantic swirl of sky-blue Crayola.

'Remember when we used to play at ghost slaying?' Sal asked her. His six-year-old self had drawn her smile so wide it didn't fit within the lines of her face. 'You used to be kinda happy.'

Asha made a non-committal noise in the back of her throat. She sat down on the carpet and looked through the rest of the drawings, half smiling.

Sal waved a hand in front of her face. 'What happened?'

'Things got weird.'

'It'll get better though, right?' Sal said. 'Now that Mum's back. Maybe you'll be able to get out more. I dunno ... see people.'

Asha turned to him with an expression of pure horror on her face. 'Oh god,' she said. 'If *you're* lecturing me on socializing then it must be bad.'

Sal snorted. 'Dirk really likes you, y'know. Maybe you could ...'

He trailed off at the sight of Asha's eyebrows, perfectly quirked into a grimace.

'He might make you happy,' he persisted. And then grumbled under his breath, 'If that's possible.'

'Sal,' Asha said carefully. 'Dirk's sweet. But there's no ... I don't know ... no magical happy ending for me here. And even if there was, it wouldn't be with him.'

★

At the very bottom of the pile of papers there were photos that Sal had never seen before. Overexposed snapshots of Dad's family in Egypt, or of their mother as a child, dressed in bright colours with wildly curling hair.

There were newer photos too. Happy times from before his dad had died and their mum had got so lost in his memory. When they had gone to museums at the weekends and to the park after school, and had parties for their birthdays.

They ended up sitting on the floor, looking through the photos one by one, forgetting the surrounding mess.

'Do you think she'll be better?' Sal asked. He had set his favourite photos to one side, ready to pin to the walls of his room. 'When she comes home?'

Asha shrugged. 'She's going to be on crutches. And have pain medication and stuff.'

'No. I mean . . .' Sal hesitated and forged forward anyway. 'About Dad? About him being gone. When she was away, she wasn't surrounded by his memory. She said she didn't feel haunted. But what if when she comes back here, it starts all over again?'

They had closed the window, but it was still very cold in the room and the wind was howling outside.

'She's promised me she'll see a counsellor,' Asha said. She attempted a smile. 'And yes, I think she gets it. That we're not really being haunted. I don't think she'll go back on that.'

Sal was quiet for a moment. Even before their dad had

257

died, their mum had often told them the house was special – full of memories. Full of ghosts. If you listened hard enough, she used to say, you could hear the voices of the people who had lived there before them. The older Asha got, the more cynical she became, but Sal couldn't help wondering if there was something in it, after all. He thought of the fight they'd all had, the day his mum had left. The truth was, he had heard that argument played back in his head, every night since. It was as if the house was holding on to it. Like it didn't want to let her go.

CHAPTER THIRTY-EIGHT

December began, and Sal returned to school, where the people who had once whispered about him in the corridors suddenly became very interested in their own shoes whenever he passed. Word had spread about his mum's car accident, and some of Dirk's old friends stopped him to ask if he was all right. One of them suggested he join the football team and looked as if he actually meant it. Aiden offered him an apologetic hand-shake and Sal managed to resist the urge to punch him all over again.

Pax had begun working his way through an astonishing variety of Christmas jumpers. Some looked as if he had knitted them himself and others were so garish that Sal could not begin to fathom where he might have found them. They came in eye-watering shades of pink or yellow or green, and were adorned with tiny bells, flashing lights and neon pom-poms.

On anyone else, Sal might have found these outfits embarrassing, but he was usually too distracted by Pax's face to give his clothing much thought. It had taken him a while to notice how good-looking he was, with his rose-bud lips and wide grey eyes. So he was making up for lost time by looking at him as much as possible.

He was so caught up in having Pax back that it took him a while to notice he was acting differently. It was disturbingly . . . *normal*. He hadn't said anything strange in days and had developed a habit of cutting himself off in the middle of sentences. Sal couldn't remember the last time he'd brought up ghosts, or witchcraft, or even vampires. He assumed it was an attempt to fit in better, and left him to it, while quietly missing his random outbursts of weirdness.

For everyone else, life seemed to go on as usual. When people weren't talking about Sal, they were talking about the winter dance. All apart from Sal, Elsie, Dirk and Pax, who sat quietly in the library without anything much to say to one another. After a full week of this, Sal cracked.

Elsie was scrawling a last-minute essay for English class, and Dirk was sitting next to her eating Monster Munch as loudly as he could and counting the number of times he could make the librarian shush him. Sal turned to Pax, who was busy doodling in the margins of a very old book with a permanent marker while playing a morose game of footsie with him under the table. None of them were smiling.

'You want to go to the dance with me?' Sal asked.

It came out louder than he had intended and the librarian looked up but forgot to tell him off, her eyes widening behind the magnifying lenses of her glasses. Dirk and Elsie's mouths dropped open in comic synchronization. Pax's pen skated across the page, leaving a thick black line across the text.

He met Sal's eye and hesitated, pointing his pen at his own chest. 'Me?'

'No,' Sal said, lowering his voice and glaring at the nosy librarian. 'The hot guy I've never spoken to before right behind you.'

Pax turned around, saw there was nobody there and flushed a bright strawberry pink. He nodded. 'Yes, please.'

'Right.' Sal folded his arms and tried not to smile. 'OK.'

Pax smiled back at him, twirling a curl of hair around his finger, head tilted to one side. Elsie returned to her essay, smirking as her pen raced across the page.

'Hang on a second,' Dirk said indignantly, looking at Sal as if he had caused him a great personal betrayal. He pointed a finger at him. 'I didn't think you'd want to go. I haven't got a date.'

'You can be my date if you want,' Elsie said, not bothering to look up from her work. 'Just don't try and kiss me or anything. That'd be really gross.'

'Yeah,' Dirk said, looking at her with renewed interest. The winter sun was pouring in through the library windows and her platinum hair was shining in the light. 'Gross.'

Sal went back to Pax's house after school. His mother was out and they started making cups of tea but ended up with Pax perched on the countertop with his legs wrapped around Sal's waist.

Sal kissed the tip of his nose, the shell of his earlobe, the sharp, pointed edges of his jaw. He hooked a finger into the fluffy fabric of his jumper and pulled it aside far enough to brush his lips over the hollows of his collarbones, and Pax melted into his touch.

At the sound of a key turning in the front door, Pax pushed him away so hard he ended up two metres away on the opposite side of the kitchen. Annie entered the kitchen, carrying half a dozen straining bags of shopping and raising her eyebrows at them suspiciously.

'Hi,' Pax said, overly brightly. He slid off the countertop. 'We were just . . . washing up.'

'I did that this morning,' Annie said, eyeing the shining (and very dry) dishes by the sink.

'We were talking,' Sal corrected, putting a few more paces between them. There was a small purple mark blooming on Pax's neck.

'I see,' Annie said, marching over and setting the bags of shopping on the countertop. She frowned down at the mugs they had left abandoned by the kettle. 'You forgot your tea,' she said.

They had put the teabags in to brew half an hour ago,

and the water had turned a deep reddish black.

'I like it strong,' Sal said.

'And cold?' she asked, picking up the mug and handing it over to him.

'Yeah.' He took a sip and tried very hard not to wince. 'Delicious.'

Annie glowered at him and he wondered if he was about to be kicked out of the house.

'Salem asked me to the dance,' Pax said, sidling up to him and linking an arm through his.

'I should think so too,' Annie said. Her tone was still grumpy, but her expression softened and she stepped forward and ruffled Sal's already quite tousled hair.

Though Annie's bad mood was evaporating, they still didn't quite dare go upstairs. They sat on the squashy sofa in the lounge instead, and Sal asked Pax to read his palm again.

'I thought you said it was bullshit,' Pax said, arching his pale blond eyebrows.

'C'mon,' Sal complained. 'Just for fun.'

He poked him in the ribs, and Pax squirmed and laughed before taking his hand, reluctantly trailing his fingers over the lines of his hands. Sal let his eyes flicker closed.

'What's your diagnosis?' he asked. When he opened his eyes, Pax was looking at his face, not his hand.

'You'll live happily ever after,' Pax said softly. 'With me, preferably.'

'Preferably,' Sal agreed.

CHAPTER THIRTY-NINE

Asha had stopped writing in the evenings, and Sal was beginning to find it disconcerting.

Instead, she sat next to him on the sofa, staring mindlessly at the television and not laughing in any of the right places. She was visiting their mum in the hospital nearly every day. Sometimes Sal went with her. They played card games, and snuck in McDonald's milkshakes and fries, because their mum couldn't stand the hospital food. She was waiting for surgery on her knee, her leg still in a brace, and her face pale from pain. But she always smiled when they got there, and made an effort to keep talking when the conversation threatened to dry up. The more effort she made, though, the more withdrawn Asha became. When Sal and Asha got home after a visit, she always looked drained.

Most concerning of all, she had started cooking. She began handing Sal plates of home-cooked food at dinner time, rather than their usual fare of frozen chicken nuggets and foil-wrapped takeaways.

She had never spent so much time with Sal, but neither had he ever seen her look quite so far away.

One Friday evening, two weeks after their mother had been rushed to hospital, he arrived home to find Asha making a roast dinner. She had left everything in the oven too long, and the house was full of the acrid scent of burning. She opened the oven door just as he stepped through into the kitchen and thick black plumes of smoke came billowing out.

'Takeaway?' Sal suggested hopefully. He was beginning to seriously miss his twice-weekly chicken chow mein with spring rolls and sweet-and-sour sauce.

'Oh.' Asha's face fell. She poked at the contents of the oven with a wooden spoon, then closed the door on it and flicked the dial off. 'Yeah, OK.'

She looked lost, and Sal was painfully reminded of their fight, when he had told her in a fit of rage that she would stay here and rot. He remembered her telling him there was no happy ending for her here. And he remembered the letter from King's College London, still hidden under the floorboard beneath his bed.

The next morning was a Saturday, and Asha's first day back at work. Sal had slept well for the first time in weeks and he awoke to find the sun was shining and Asha had already left. He left the house just before midday, after a breakfast of cold noodles and leftover prawn crackers.

Dirk's house had a Christmas tree in the window. Walking down the street towards it, Sal felt as though he had entered a parallel world, in which everything was inappropriately festive and bright. The red-bricked houses had all been adorned with lights, and signs saying *Santa Stop Here* were staked in every other lawn. There were children playing on scooters at the end of the road.

When Dirk opened the door, he was dressed for football practice and still splattered with mud. At the sight of Sal, he grinned and swung the door wider for him to enter.

'Hey,' he said. 'How's it going?'

Sal had brought back the coat that Dirk had lent to Asha at the hospital. It was neatly folded and smelt of fresh washing powder.

'She washed it,' Sal said, handing it over. 'I think she was worried that you never would.'

'You're not funny,' Dirk said, taking the jacket and slinging it over the banisters.

'I'm not joking,' Sal said.

Dirk's mum stuck her head out of the kitchen behind him, and then came rushing over, arms outstretched. Sal had been on the receiving end of a great deal of unwelcome impromptu hugs over the past few days. But he had always liked Mrs Madden, so he was willing to tolerate it. Mr Madden passed them in the hallway and gave Sal an apologetic nod over his wife's shoulder.

'Let him go, Mum,' Dirk said impatiently. 'He's fine.'

She ended the hug and Sal tried to pull an appreciative face, which felt like it came out as more of a grimace. He let Dirk drag him towards the stairs.

'Well, OK then,' she called after them. She waved, looking as if she would dearly like to follow them and subject them both to more emotional embraces. 'Good to see you, Sal.'

'She got in?' Dirk said, when Sal produced the letter from King's and waved it under his nose. 'Again, I mean?'

They had settled on the bed in Dirk's room with Grey sprawled out between them, drooling on to Sal's jeans and staring up at him with mournful eyes.

'Yeah.' Sal grinned. He pushed Grey's head off his lap and helped himself to Dirk's laptop. 'They said she can start in January. I'm gonna book her accommodation so she can't say no.'

'But what about your mum?' Dirk asked, turning the letter over with a sceptical frown on his face.

'She'll be back by then,' Sal said. He took the letter back and typed in the web address listed at the top. 'They said she might be able to come home next week.'

'That's great,' Dirk said. 'No more parental freedom, though, eh?'

Sal hummed vaguely. He hadn't felt free when his mum had left. Mostly, he'd just felt lost. Though he wouldn't admit it, he was looking forward to having her back.

Dirk was watching as Sal flicked through photos of

university accommodation, frowning at the prices beneath them. There was inheritance left from their grandparents. He knew that. And the money his mum had made from her early paintings. But he didn't know if it would cover *this*.

'You do know she can get a loan, right?' Dirk asked, in an unusual flash of perceptiveness. 'And there are, like, grants and stuff you can apply for too.'

'Huh,' Sal said. He opened up another tab and began googling.

'Why are you doing all of this for her, anyway?'

Sal shrugged. 'She deserves it.'

Asha had been looking after him for as long as he could remember. He had let her try to fill a space that was far too big for her. And she'd done it. Of course she had. Asha could do anything. But she'd poured every tiny part of herself into keeping him happy, and not left anything over for herself.

It felt like it was time to return the favour.

'Won't you miss her if she goes?' Dirk asked, absent-mindedly rubbing Grey behind the ears.

Sal raised an eyebrow at him. 'Not as much as you will.'

He expected Dirk to laugh, but he didn't. He was reclining against the pillows, staring up at the ceiling with a furrowed brow.

'Nah,' he said eventually. 'You were right. The way I've been obsessing over her . . . It *is* pathetic. You're my best mate and I should have been on your side. I love you more than her, dude.'

'Oh god,' Sal said. 'What am I gonna tell Pax?'

Dirk punched him on the arm. 'You know what I mean.'

'She said you're sweet,' Sal said, then instantly regretted it when Dirk's eyes lit up.

'Really?'

Sal hurried to correct himself. 'But, like . . . in the same way she talks about the mouse that's been hiding in our kitchen cupboards.'

'Right,' Dirk said, frowning. He took in a deep breath. 'The thing is . . . I don't think I *really* love her. I think I just love the idea of her, y'know?'

Sal snorted. 'Is that a poetic way of saying you just like her face?'

'Well.' Dirk grinned. 'Not *just* her face.'

Sal hit him around the head with a pillow.

'I'm glad we're back to normal,' Dirk said.

'Yeah,' Sal said. He hit him again for good measure. 'Me too.'

CHAPTER FORTY

As soon as Sal got through the door that evening, he raced upstairs and retrieved the King's prospectus from Asha's desk drawer. He left it on the kitchen table, open at the page on English Literature. He unfolded the letter he had received, attempted to flatten out the creases and left it next to it.

Two minutes later, Asha's key turned in the door, and Sal resisted the urge to dive under the kitchen table in fear. He stood watching the door, tugging the ends of his hoodie sleeves down over his hands.

When Asha entered the room, her face went blank at the sight of the prospectus on the table. Then it contorted with anger. 'You've been in my room.'

She said it as if Sal had personally invaded her mind. Which, he supposed, he kind of had.

'Yeah, that was months ago,' he said. 'Read the letter.'

Asha picked up the letter as if it might be about to explode. She looked at Sal with such suspicion that he couldn't help grinning. Holding it at arm's length, she squinted her way through the first few lines. She let out a great breath of air all at once through her nose, set the letter back down on the table, turned her back on him and flicked on the kettle.

'I can't go, Sal,' she said.

'You have to,' Sal said. 'I've booked your accommodation.'

'Yeah?' She opened the cupboard and pulled out two mugs, keeping her back to him. 'Did you get an en suite?'

'Duh.'

She laughed, burrowing her head in her hands as she turned back around to face him. 'You can't just go around pretending to be other people, Sal.'

'It doesn't count,' Sal said. 'You're my sister. We're a team.'

'*Exactly*,' she said. 'We're a team. I can't just waltz off and leave you on your own. I don't *want* to leave you on your own.'

'I won't be on my own,' Sal protested. 'Mum will be back soon. And I've got Dirk and Elsie. And Pax.'

Asha smiled when he mentioned Pax's name. It was an annoying habit she'd developed over the past few weeks, and it always made Sal grumpy which, in turn, just made her smile even more.

'The doctors said Mum's only going to be in the hospital for a few more days,' he continued, addressing the table so he didn't have to see her incessant smirking. 'She'll be back way before you'd have to leave. And it's only an hour away. You can come back and see us on the weekends.'

'But what if Mum takes off again?' Asha asked quietly.

Sal shook his head. 'What if she doesn't? Are you really gonna spend the rest of your life waiting to see what *Mum* does? What about what you want to do?'

Asha looked like she was faltering. 'You and Mum are a disaster combination.' She bit her lip. 'You won't do the hoovering.'

'No,' Sal agreed. 'We'll probably die from dust inhalation.'

'Or poison yourselves. Neither of you can cook.'

'Neither can you,' he said. The bottom of the oven was still black with burnt chicken fat.

'Ah, but I'm scrappy and self-sufficient,' she said. 'I'm a natural survivor.'

'So am I,' Sal said, scowling.

'No, you're not. You're my baby brother,' she said softly, looking misty-eyed. She smirked again and ruined the moment. 'You're the runt of the litter.'

Sal thought this was a little rich, coming from a girl who barely reached five feet high and was roughly the width of a pencil. He glared at her.

'You're going. It's non-negotiable.'

'Fine,' she said. She picked up the letter again and smiled and then laughed. It wasn't her usual short sarcastic bark. She laughed properly, like the sound was being drawn up out of her and she had no other choice but to let it go. 'I'm going.'

'Great.' Sal turned to leave.

'But you *have* to tell me if anything happens,' she said, grabbing him by the arm before he could safely vacate the room.

She was still clutching the letter in her left hand and she looked back down at it, hands shaking slightly. 'And you'll have to call me every day.'

'OK.'

'And I'll come back every weekend.'

'Fine.'

Asha was looking at him like it was the last time she'd ever see him. 'And for the holidays.'

'I'll be sick of seeing you,' Sal lied.

'Yeah.' She pulled him into a suffocating hug. 'Ditto.'

Their mum came home three days later. Sal got back from school to find her climbing out of a taxi, still on crutches, with Asha at her side. She seemed determined to prove things had changed, and Sal could tell she was making an effort – helping to cook dinners and clean, despite being on crutches. She asked questions about school, and university, and everything else she'd missed. She didn't mention their dad, although Sal occasionally caught her looking sad and faraway when she thought he wasn't looking.

They had a belated birthday celebration for Asha a couple of days after her return. Their mum ordered a cake from the local bakery, and gave Asha a brand-new laptop to take to uni – a sleek silver one that didn't make a loud whirring noise whenever it was turned on.

Things were awkward at first though, while they learnt how to fit together again. Asha and his mum were tiptoeing around each other – both being overly polite and going out of their way to be helpful. It took them getting into an argument over who was doing the washing-up (their mum was trying to do it on crutches, and Asha trying to take over) before things felt normal again. Sal rushed downstairs at the sound of shouting, only to find the argument had already ended, and they were both covered in soapsuds, and doubled over with laughter.

Asha threw a handful of soapsuds at him when he stuck his head around the kitchen door, and he ducked away to hide his smile.

CHAPTER FORTY-ONE

Asha was staring at him. Weirdly.

'It doesn't fit right, does it?' Sal said.

The suit trousers were a few centimetres too short in the leg and the jacket felt tight across his shoulders. He'd tried on a tie, but had removed it again after deciding he looked like a businessman. Then he'd undone his top shirt button and messed his hair up as much as possible, as a protest against the formal dress code.

'No,' Asha said. 'No, it fits fine. I just . . . you look . . . *nice*.'

'Huh,' Sal said grumpily. It was the night of the school dance and his stomach kept tilting with nerves. 'Thanks for sounding surprised about it.'

'No problem.'

Asha continued to stare at him until he stuck his

tongue out, and she rolled her eyes and returned to her book. She was sprawled on the sofa in the living room, making a start on her university reading list for the upcoming term. She had lit the fire and the room felt less gloomy than usual. Sal could see his own reflection in the newly sparkling windows, behind which night had fallen and the occasional flake of snow was beginning to drift down.

The doorbell rang and Sal nervously ran a hand through his hair. Asha sprang to her feet and tried to dive past him to answer it. He picked her up, threw her back on the sofa and went to answer it himself.

He met his mum in the hallway, emerging from the kitchen on her crutches and heading for the door. She smiled at the sight of him in his suit, and he grimaced at her, diving round her to get to the door first.

'Wow,' Pax said, as soon as Sal opened the door, his eyes even wider than usual. He looked him up and down, mouth open. 'You should dress like that all the time.'

He had brought Annie along, and she was looking at Pax as though he were the eighth wonder of the world.

Sal was inclined to agree with her.

It had been stupid, he realized, to expect Pax to wear a black-and-white tux. He was wearing a floral-patterned suit with a crisp white shirt, shiny black shoes and a length of green velvet ribbon tied into a rough approximation of a bow tie around his neck. But it was the first time Sal had ever seen him out of knitwear, and he considered this something of a victory.

He stepped back to let them inside, and Pax scooted immediately past, catching sight of Sal's mum still hovering in the hallway behind him.

'Hello,' he said, shaking her hand, so vigorously he caused her to wobble on her crutches. 'I've been dying to meet you for ages.'

'He has,' Asha agreed cheerfully, sticking her head out of the living room doorway.

His mum hesitated, obviously confused.

'This is Pax,' Sal said.

His mum didn't know about Pax. He'd been meaning to tell her about him ever since she'd come home, but it had never quite seemed like the right time. When he had agreed to Pax coming over before the dance, he'd been half hoping he could slip out of the door without making any introductions. He hadn't counted on Pax arriving half an hour too early to actually set off. Or on him bringing Annie with him.

'And this is his mum, Annie,' he said, folding his arms defensively as Annie beamed and waved at his mum.

She had brought a very large camera with her, and wasted no time in ushering them out into the garden where she made them stand in the snow while she snapped photo after photo until Pax had started shivering and, as Sal pointed out, the ends of his fingers were turning blue.

She finally let them back inside and insisted on taking yet more photos of them in front of the fireplace. Sal was finding it difficult to relax. His mum was leaning in the doorway watching them, and he saw the flicker of surprise pass over her face when Pax slipped his arm around Sal's waist.

She followed him into the kitchen when he went to grab a glass of water before he and Pax left for the dance.

'You and Pax seem very close,' she said pointedly.

'Yeah,' Sal said. He stopped filling his glass and turned to face her. 'He's my boyfriend.'

His mum clenched her jaw, her brow furrowing.

'You're upset,' he said.

'Yes,' she agreed.

Sal swallowed. She was watching him, and he felt dizzyingly, painfully visible. He wanted, suddenly, nothing more than to disappear. It occurred to him he wasn't prepared for this conversation.

'I didn't think you would be,' he said. He left his glass on the side, unfilled, and moved past her, towards the door.

'I'm not upset that he's your boyfriend,' his mum said. She reached out to stop him. 'I'm upset I wasn't here to meet him sooner.'

She pulled him into a hug, and the sensation of relief was so immensely overpowering that Sal felt tears run down his own cheeks and sink into the material of her jumper.

He pulled away and scrubbed at his face, furiously. 'It's fine,' he said. 'It doesn't matter.'

'Then why are you crying?' his mum asked, half smiling.

'I'm not,' Sal said.

'It does matter,' his mum said. She squeezed his shoulders, her hands warm through his suit jacket. 'I'll make it up to you, Sal.'

Sal was careful to scrub the tears off his face before returning to the living room, but Pax's brow still furrowed with concern when he walked in. He mouthed *are you OK?* at him and Sal nodded, reaching for his hand.

'Ready?' Pax asked. 'It's time to go.'

They left Annie with Sal's mum in the living room, opening a bottle of wine and getting along alarmingly well. It seemed to Sal like a terrible idea to leave them alone together, but Pax didn't appear to share his concerns. He dragged him out of the house and told him to walk quickly or they'd be late.

The lane was lit only by the glow of light falling from the windows of the cottages that lined it. On the walk to school, tiny flakes of snow continued to fall. The last of the autumn leaves were still rotting on the ground, but they had frozen when the sun set, and they crumbled into icy shards beneath their feet. Everything was grey and shadowy, but someone had lined the path through the woods with fairy lights, which glistened like golden fireflies in the dark.

'This is so cliched, I might vomit,' Sal said.

Pax just smiled. 'I think it's pretty. I feel like I'm in one of your old movies.'

As they approached the school, the illusion vanished. The dance was being held in the sixth-form cafeteria, and it still looked very much like a cafeteria, only with all the tables pushed to the sides of the room to form a scuffed and sticky makeshift dance floor. The ceiling was draped with spangly banners made from tinsel and yet more fairy lights. It would, Sal thought, have benefitted dramatically from Elsie's ice sculpture. The music playing was the sort that always made Sal reach out and turn the radio off, and the room was filled with laughing, dancing people.

'You sure you wanna go in there?' Sal asked. He wrinkled his nose up against the smell of greasy pizza, which still filled the room.

At his side, Pax was looking through the doors as if he were standing at the gates to heaven. He grabbed Sal's hand and pulled him inside.

CHAPTER FORTY-TWO

They found Dirk and Elsie standing in the far corner. They were strategically positioned next to a bowl of punch, which appeared to consist primarily of red gloop, fruit cocktail and (if Dirk was to be believed) an entire bottle of vodka, courtesy of the football team.

Elsie was dressed in a long silvery dress that shone in the light. Her blonde hair had been artfully arranged in a bun at the nape of her neck. She was carrying a beaded clutch bag which, it soon transpired, was hiding a surprisingly large bottle of peach schnapps. Dirk was wearing a very smart suit with a too-loose tie and a scruffy pair of trainers. They were already bickering when Sal and Pax joined them, but still looked like they were having a better time than all of the couples wrapped around each other on the dance floor.

'You two are ridiculous,' Sal told them.

'At least we're not in love,' Dirk said, voice accusatory.

Sal didn't really know what to say to that, so he ignored him and helped himself to a drink. At his side, Pax had turned the same colour as the punch.

Pretending not to notice, Sal looked out across the room. People, for once, weren't paying him any attention, all too wrapped up in their partners or friends to notice any outsiders. Everyone was drinking the punch, including Mr Gulliver. He was swaying slightly on his feet, looking rosy-cheeked and happier than Sal had ever seen him. He waved when he saw Sal looking and gave him an exaggeratedly encouraging thumbs up from across the room.

At the other end of the room, Jacob and Aiden were standing in the middle of a large group of people who all looked very drunk. Aiden, who never had anything intelligent to say, was shouting something that left the rest of the group in hysterics. Jacob had a girl hanging off his arm. It was one of Elsie's old friends. They all looked deeply, infuriatingly happy.

The thing about people like Jacob and Aiden, Sal thought, was that they were really, seriously uncool. But because *they* hadn't noticed, somehow nobody else had either.

'How come the worst people get the best luck?' he asked.

'You want to be like them?' Elsie asked him, following his gaze. Her lip curled at the sight of Jacob.

'No, thanks.'

'Right,' Elsie agreed. 'Because they *don't* have the best luck. They just think they do and one day they're gonna wake up and realize they don't like the people they've become. Or they won't. Either way, Sal, they're not winning.'

'Neither am I,' Sal said.

'But at least you're in the running.'

'And he's a fast runner,' Dirk chipped in.

'Yeah,' Sal agreed, feeling marginally more cheerful. 'I can run.'

'When are we going to dance?' Pax asked an hour later, wrapping his arms around Sal's waist from behind. He had disappeared with Elsie and her bottle of schnapps and come back extremely giggly and even more exuberant than usual.

'I don't dance,' Sal said. He and Dirk had found a table of snacks and were working their way through a bowl of peanuts.

'You *asked me* to a dance,' Pax protested, stepping back and poking him deep in the ribs. 'It would be rude not to.'

Sal hadn't thought of that. Startled, he glanced at Elsie for clarification. 'Would it?'

She nodded, grabbed Dirk by the hands and pulled him on to the dance floor. They disappeared amid the crowd. The music had slowed down and everyone was tightly entwined with their partners.

'Oh god,' Sal said, as Pax's hands found his own and tugged. 'Fine.'

He allowed himself to be dragged into the midst of the dancers. In a slight state of panic, he wrapped his arms around Pax's waist. Pax looked up at him, eyes sparkling in the light, and his hands slipped up over Sal's chest and linked behind his neck.

'I knew you'd secretly be a romantic,' he said cheerfully.

Sal scowled back at him. He pulled him closer so that their chests were pressed together and Pax was forced to stop talking and rest his face against Sal's neck. They swayed in time with the music, and Sal was surprised to realize it wasn't the worst thing that had ever happened to him.

It was actually quite nice, having Pax pressed against him from head to toe. And even nicer because it was expected of them. No one had even glanced at them since they started dancing. Sal looked down at the boy in his arms, and let everything else fade into blissful non-existence, until he was unaware of everyone else around them, and the ceiling above their heads, and the floor beneath their feet. He was halfway through this thought when it occurred to him that he might have overdone the punch, just a little.

Three songs in, Pax lifted his head from Sal's shoulder. He tilted his chin up and looked at him expectantly. Sal forgot to check if anyone was watching. He leant in, unthinkingly, and met his lips in a kiss.

'You two have no shame,' Elsie said, interrupting them within seconds. She was pink in the face from dancing and her hair was breaking free of its bun, in loose flyaway tendrils that framed her face. 'You're in public.'

'Not sure you're one to talk about doing things in public, Elsie,' said a crowing voice from behind her.

Aiden and Jacob were walking past. Jacob cackled at Aiden's words, and they raised their hands and high-fived each other in self-satisfied glee.

Elsie and Sal moved at exactly the same time. His hand came up and fastened around Aiden's throat, just as Elsie's fist collided with Jacob's nose. Behind them, Pax was squealing at Sal to stop and Dirk was shouting at Elsie to keep going. She punched Jacob again and, when he moved to hit her back, ducked so quickly that his fist collided with Dirk behind her. There was a sickening crunch as Jacob's fist met his jaw, and Dirk launched himself forward, sending Jacob, the people around him and the table holding the punch toppling to the floor.

The glass bowl hit the floor with a crash and shattered into a thousand glittering shards. The linoleum floor was awash with a sticky red sea. Sal released Aiden's throat, and Aiden staggered backwards, before losing his footing and falling to lie flat on his back.

Pax's arms fastened around Sal's waist to prevent him from toppling with him, and he found himself being dragged away towards the nearest fire exit. They stumbled past Mr Gulliver as they went, who was close enough to stop them, but moving determinedly in Jacob's direction. Elsie overtook them mid-escape, and flung the doors open, through which they tumbled out into the night.

The three of them ran together, hand in hand, across

the stone courtyard and down on to the playing fields beyond. They collapsed, as one, in a heap on the white-frosted bank overlooking the woods and descended into breathless, adrenaline-fuelled laughter.

It was snowing harder and, behind them, the muddy outlines of their footprints were already being filled in. Sal had sobered up in the cold night air and, even without the haze of vodka to cloud his judgement, things felt good.

'Oh no,' Pax gasped out. His hands were clasped to his face in shock. 'Oh no. Oh no. Mum's going to kill me.'

'No, she won't,' Sal said, feeling a stab of regret. His good mood evaporated. Annie had trusted him and he had ruined Pax's perfect night. He couldn't imagine she'd forgive him. 'She'll kill *me*.'

'I can't believe Mr Gulliver just let us go,' Pax said. 'I ran right into him.'

'I think he's on our side,' Elsie said, smirking.

They were interrupted by the sound of someone huffing their way towards them across the grass. Elsie lifted her head to look. She had water marks from the snow on her dress, and her hair had fallen out of its delicate up-do and was cascading in tangled waves down to the ground.

'Jesus,' Dirk complained, approaching them. He was panting, soaked in punch and still clutching his jaw. 'Don't wait for your hero or anything.'

He sank on to the ground at Elsie's side.

'You're not my hero,' Elsie said, punching him lightly on the arm.

'No,' he agreed. He picked up her clenched fist and eyed it in admiration. There was blood on his own hands from where he'd landed on broken glass. 'You didn't really need one, huh?'

CHAPTER FORTY-THREE

The four of them walked home together through the woods, stopping every few minutes so that Dirk could ice his jaw with snow and swear profusely. The fairy lights looked dimmer, their batteries failing. When they reached Pax's house, Elsie and Dirk waved goodbye and disappeared off in the same direction, despite living at opposite ends of the village.

Pax's house looked incredibly welcoming through the snow. In the front windows shone the flickering light of a fire blazing in the fireplace. They could see Annie in the kitchen, flicking through recipe books by the stove. Sal tensed at the sight of her.

'We got in a fight,' Pax blurted out as soon as they were through the front door.

Annie did not look particularly surprised by this

exclamation, and Sal supposed she had grown used to Pax word-vomiting his secrets as soon as he set eyes on her. She raised an eyebrow and looked them up and down. Pax had snow strewn through his hair, and Sal's shirt was splashed pink with punch. Their shoes were caked in mud from running across the school grounds.

She folded her arms and drew herself up to her full height. She was still a good head shorter than Sal but, combined with her stern expression, it was enough to make him feel intimidated.

'It wasn't Pax,' he said. 'It was my fault.'

'He was being heroic again,' Pax said, placing a protective hand on Sal's chest.

This did not go down well with Annie. Her eyes narrowed and she glowered at them from across the room.

'I'll go,' Sal said, his ears burning and his throat tight. He squeezed Pax's hand and carefully removed it from his chest, then turned to the door.

'Don't be ridiculous, Salem,' Annie said, voice stern.

He turned back around, confused.

'You get one free pass,' she said. '*One*. Then I'll be obliged to disapprove of you.'

Sal swallowed and nodded. 'That sounds fair.'

She clanked a pan down on the stove and began opening a bottle of mulled wine.

'And you get a bonus point for bringing him home before midnight.'

Sal leant sideways and checked the clock on the wall behind her. It was 10.57.

'Can I get two for bringing him home before eleven?' he asked hopefully.

'I'm not a parcel,' Pax complained behind them.

'Of course you're not, sweetheart,' Annie said. She turned back to Sal. 'And *no*. Don't push your luck.'

They went up to Pax's room and Sal did a double take when they went through the door. Half of the shelves had been swept clean. His crystals had gone. His tarot cards were nowhere to be seen. The books on supernatural occurrences had disappeared. It felt oddly bare, and Pax looked embarrassed and shrugged when Sal asked him about it.

He waited until Annie called Pax downstairs and then rummaged through every nook and cranny in the room until he found what he was looking for. Pax had boxed up everything remotely ghost-related and stashed it in the cramped, dusty space beneath the bed. Sal unboxed it and put everything back out on to the shelves, one by one: the feathered charms; the slabs of granite; the leather-bound books; the sparkling chunks of amethyst; the spangled amulets. When he was finished the room felt like Pax's again. He wrapped himself in the patchwork quilt and helped himself to one of the vampire romances from the bookshelf.

When Pax came back, he was pink-cheeked and carrying two glasses of mulled wine, complete with thick slices of orange and cinnamon sticks as stirrers. He glanced around the room. His eyes fell on the line of crystals on the bookshelf. He set the glasses down on the bedside table so suddenly that the wine sloshed out and on to the wood. Then he snatched the book out of Sal's hands, mouth set in a pink rosebud pout.

'You searched my room.'

'Yeah,' Sal said. 'You'd hidden all your weird stuff. I thought it was a treasure hunt.'

Pax made a little noise of confusion in the back of his throat, his nose wrinkling. 'I don't understand. I thought you didn't like my weird stuff.'

Sal frowned. 'I love your weird stuff.'

'You put the crystals back in the wrong order,' Pax said, but he was smiling. He sank down on to the bed at Sal's side and stole half of the patchwork quilt. 'You'll unbalance my energy.'

'You're already unbalanced,' Sal teased. 'Why did you hide everything?'

Pax sighed, fidgeting with the green velvet ribbon around his collar. He tugged it looser. 'I just wanted to be more normal for you. I thought you deserved that.'

Sal pulled him closer. 'I don't want you to be normal. And I don't want you to be anything *for* me. I want you to be who you want to be.'

'But you have enough weird stuff in your life.'

'Maybe weird *is* my normal,' Sal said.

Pax's mouth twitched into a smile, his nose wrinkling. 'I think it's mine too.'

The house was very warm, and the night outside was very black. Pax leant into him, head resting on his chest.

'Why didn't you tell me?' he asked. 'About your mum?'

There was no hint of accusation in his words, but Sal could tell he was still hurting. He tried to answer, but the words got stuck in the back of his throat.

'Why didn't you tell me, Salem?' Pax repeated, his voice breaking.

'I couldn't,' Sal said. He buried his nose in Pax's hair. 'I'm sorry.'

Pax lifted his head to meet his eye. 'Can you tell me now?'

Sal opened his mouth to say he *couldn't* and then, out of nowhere, found that he could. The story had been pulsing in his chest since he was a child, locked in the dark secret space behind the cage of his ribs. He told Pax about his past. About the day his father had died, and how it felt like they had lost their mum that day too. About the times they had all been so desperate for him to come home that living in a haunted house had felt like a blessing. The times Sal, like his mum, had convinced himself his dad was still there.

He told him all the things that hadn't gone into Asha's article. The memories that were his and his alone, and that he had kept shut away since they were made. He told him the truth about Asha too. How she had made things work. And occasionally even work well. How she had pulled their family together, not ripped it apart. How much he would miss her when she was gone.

When he had finished, he felt lighter. So light he could nearly float away. And he was hungry. It was nearly midnight but the smell of Annie's baking was floating up the stairs. Pax did not speak. He was gripping his hand, and staring at him with his soft, forgiving eyes. There was a flicker of something else too. Something darker, something haunted.

'You want to light some sage?' Sal asked. 'Scare away some ghosts?'

Pax smiled and sank down to lie next to him. 'I'd like that.'

'Yeah,' Sal said. He laced their fingers together. 'Me too.'

It was past midnight by the time Sal left Pax's house. Snow was still falling in soft flurries as he walked up the lane, flecking the shoulders of his suit jacket in a sparkling white. The cold was sharp enough to bite at the exposed skin of his face and neck. Jumping the gate on to his own driveway, he looked up to see Asha and his mum had left the lights on. Warm orange light spilt from every window, and the heavy sense of dread Sal had come to associate with the house lifted a touch.

He approached the front door to find a fresh wreath of lavender hanging from the handle. He ran a finger over it and it crumbled beneath his fingers, descending to the ground in a silvery dust so fine that it looked as if it hadn't really been there at all.

Despite Asha's insistence that ghosts didn't exist, Sal had always thought there was something strange about their house. He remembered the piece of jet that had mysteriously reappeared underneath his pillow. The way the last lavender wreath had appeared around his wrist in the night. Inexplicable occurrences that he thought should probably have scared him, but that didn't at all. Whether ghosts lived inside or not, he no longer felt haunted.

It was a weird house, he thought. But, for the first time in years, he was glad to be home.

ACKNOWLEDGEMENTS

Thank you to Kesia Lupo, whose belief in this book quite literally changed my life. You saw something in *The Other Ones* the first time you read it, and have been kind enough to champion it ever since. Working with you on this novel has been an absolute dream and I don't think *The Other Ones* could have found a better home.

Thanks also to the judges on the 2020 *Times*/Chicken House Children's Fiction Competition panel: Camilla Borthwick, Emma Bradshaw, Kiran Millwood Hargrave, Alex O'Connell and Trudi Tweedie. I am a little in awe of every one of you, and was completely overwhelmed to hear that you had enjoyed my book.

An extra-special thank you to Barry Cunningham for picking *The Other Ones* as your Chairman's Choice that year. What an honour! I hope it's become the book you thought it could be.

To the incredible Chicken House team: Rachel Leyshon, Rachel Hickman, Elinor Bagenal, Esther Waller, Laura Myers, Sarah Wallis-Newman, Olivia Jeggo and Jazz Bartlett Love. Thank you for helping to bring this book into the world. I think you're all the coolest.

Thanks also to Micaela Alcaino, for bringing my characters to life in her stunning cover design.

To my amazing agent, Kate Shaw. I feel very lucky to have had you to guide me through such a strange time. Your advice is always impeccable, and you brought so much to this story.

My family is my safety net, without which I never would have felt brave enough to release this book into the world. To my amazing mum, for being my first choice of person to go to when things get tough (sorry about that!). There have never been hard times that you weren't able to make at least a little bit easier. To Badger, for keeping me grounded, and for always being confused when I thought I couldn't do this. And to Buffy. You're the absolute cutest.

To Caroline – you are my favourite person, and always will be. Your strength inspires me every day. It also inspired some of Asha's epic big-sister energy. She is my favourite character, and that's partly because she reminds me a little of you.

And, last but not least, to anyone who has picked up this book and given it a chance. I wrote *The Other Ones* for myself, and never dreamt it would fall into your hands. But I'm so glad it finally did, and I hope you enjoyed the read.